RUTHLESS POSITIVITY

AVERY BLAKE

STERLING & STONE

RUTHLESS POSITIVITY

Chapter One

Kam

KAM WANTED to murder her inner voice.

But there she was like always. Julia Grace, planting a flag inside her mind. Or digging a trench might be more like it. Kam kept trying to claw her way out, and Julia, fiend that she was, kept stepping on Kam's fingers, grinding a heel into her knuckles, and waiting for her to fall.

Not that Julia Grace even knew who Kam was. It didn't matter that Kam's father had frittered every precious credit buying drums of the woman's snake oil. He was just one of millions who believed in her bullshit. And Kam was but one of millions of her victims.

She would do anything to silence the voice, but there it was again:

To get the best possible life for yourself, you need to expect it.

Kam didn't want to hear the next part, but it burrowed up from the nooks and crannies of her brain anyway.

You must be ruthlessly positive, Julia finished. *Nothing else will do.*

But Kam wasn't feeling especially ruthless or positive. Right now she just longed to feel normal. Staying present was hard enough, the way her mind had a way of always wandering off. It took her a long time to find the kind of friends (if that's what these were) she needed inside eScape, the least Kam could do was listen to what they were saying.

She should be fine. The Malt Shoppe was her safe place. Kam came here as often as she could, always sitting in the same booth, right in the beating heart of the place, because yesterday never mattered in that special spot, and it never would. That's why the Malt Shoppe was Kam's favorite haunt in the virtual playground known as eScape.

The Malt Shoppe was a hot spot, always packed with people and vibrantly alive with conversation. Everything in the place was oversized. The furniture, the giant cushions, even the dishes and utensils adhered to the exaggerated aesthetic. Order a shake and it came with a glass big enough for an entire table to share, plus a metal cup for a fill-up after the thing was finished. Best of all, Kam could drink as many shakes as she wanted, and eat burgers and fries by the bucket. She never got sick. Not here.

The Malt Shoppe created a kind of timeless vibe, borrowing from the 1950s as much as it leaned into the modern look that colored the world a century later. A massive screen swallowed the back wall, broadcasting from the rear of the Shoppe, letting all the diners inside know everything from weather conditions outside eScape — that always seemed awfully silly to Kam, because who would ever want to be reminded about the world outside when inside here? — to which of its biggest and brightest stars might be offering exclusive access for eScape credits. The Shoppe was always gleaming, from silver piping around the signage to spigots on the soda fountain, all of it a reminder of how clean everything was in here, and how happy Kam could sometimes convince herself she was around what felt like emotional polish.

Her friends were beautiful in here, but so was she. Kam's usual booth was the best, perfectly situated so she could admire both her friends and their surroundings. Glancing up at the burnished steel wall, she could praise her reflection; something that could never happen outside. In here she was strong, beautiful, and perhaps even beguiling. Deserving of her peers and welcome around them. Out there she felt like a walking disease.

Kam was doing what she usually did, listening to the conversation at their table, while also tuning into as many of the surrounding exchanges as she could. Kelso and Dee had most of her attention, which made sense since they were talking about money. That particular subject never dulled for Kam. Of course she knew that credits weren't everything, but that didn't change the cold hard truth that both worlds required credits to run.

"I only want three houses," Dee continued. "I feel like it's time to finally let go of some things."

"You could always keep the houses, but rent them out to the lessers," Kelso suggested.

"Gross." Dee made a face.

Raquel vigorously nodded. "Lessers are *so* dirty."

Kelso said, "What do you care, if you're only doing it to keep the credits?"

When you had as much money in the real world as Kam's three friends, or at least as much as their families had, eScape credits came cheap. Dee had been buying property inside the digital paradise that she didn't need and could barely even use.

Kam looked around the Malt Shoppe, not bothering to

hear Dee's response. The conversation could continue without her. Dee would say something even more spoiled, of course. She always did. Kam would rather study the crowd. She was still in awe of this place, and always would be. At least she hoped so. It would be awful to lose her respect and take it all for granted, just like her so-called friends already had. They were born rich and would die even richer. Their lives were a luxury, from the clothes they wore and the cars they drove, to the AI assistants that helped them run such privileged existences.

Studying the customers, Kam saw only two people who looked like they might be over thirty, an older couple sitting all the way across the Shoppe. At a glance, they might have been twice as old as anyone else in the place, from sippers to servers. Though avatars could lie when a user needed them to, and that was a truth she intimately understood.

Kam wondered how many credits were in her account, and whether there were more than when she woke up that morning, or less. The Malt Shoppe was her home base within eScape, but it was more than that as well. In some ways, the spot was everything.

Her friends were all rich, and Kam got off on the fact that she had fooled them into thinking she was one of them. The deception wasn't exactly part of her plan. It just sort of happened, one little lie at a time. It's what she needed, to stop wanting to die.

Kelso, Dee, and Raquel — none of her eScape compatriots had a clue that she'd grown up with pieces missing from her squalid apartment's walls. Neither did their AI assistants. Thanks to Pibly, the baseline auxiliary she could barely afford, but had hacked into doing her bidding. None of them had any idea that she was a dying girl, raised in the rundowns by an abusive, schizophrenic father.

She tolerated the boasting, all that bragging about their

homes in Elysium, diamond bracelets, excursions on a yacht, or all-day trips to The Tranquil Garden — eScape's most expensive spa where customers were treated like royalty, getting cream rubbed into their skin with crushed pearls and colloidal gold until their skin looked even more radiant inside the digital artifice than it did outside, and unplugged from their Nest.

Such discussions once made her feel lost, and kept Kam from feeling like she mattered at all. She had a better handle on it now, knowing that the best of the artificial world belonged to her. In eScape, Kam could live like the obscenely rich, as long as she kept her thieving invisible, while possessing a perspective that set her far apart from everyone else.

Still, sometimes the conversations could become too much and Kam had to tune out her friends or risk their empty words spilling acid into her stomach.

They were discussing endless credits like usual, but the character of their exchange had withered to something even worse than before. The volley started with the usual banter among the three of them, as Kam mostly listened.

Pibly was listening too, waiting for the perfectly appropriate moment to drop either insight or whimsy. AIs weren't supposed to have a sense of humor, but that particular hack had felt especially important. Each of Kam's friends was awful in their own way, but she had to admit that despite them being rich and selfish and totally out of touch, they also made her envy all they had and couldn't possibly appreciate.

In the last ten minutes alone each of her friends had said something unintentionally obnoxious.

Kelso: "Money doesn't make you happy. My parents have almost a hundred million, most of that made in the last ten years, and they swear they're not any happier than they were at fifty."

Dee: "We had three maids, but four really seemed to fit our lifestyle better."

Raquel: "Daddy won't let me use the jet this summer. He says I travel enough inside eScape."

Her friends kept measuring wallets, digital and otherwise, until the conversation turned even more patronizing, and a lot more personal.

Raquel said, "It really is hard to get good help. It's like their brains are different than ours."

"No kidding," Kelso agreed.

Then Dee. "It's not your fault if you're born poor, but it sure the hell is if you die that way."

Raquel nodded, rolling her eyes to further the insult. "If everyone would just work harder to become their best selves, then they would be able to manifest whatever they wanted in life. A good life comes from positive thinking."

Now Kam was dying to say something, but still she couldn't. So she kept chewing on her lip while nodding, implying consent even though the truth of it all seemed obvious to her. The system was rigged in favor of those already at the top. Always had been, always would be.

Her friends wouldn't want to hear what she had to say, and Kam wasn't dumb enough to soil her chances. Life had given them their perspective, same as hers. She didn't need to participate in the discussion. Kam reminded herself that she was smart, that she was slowly beating the system, and that she was nothing like the lessers her friends were all shitting on.

"Ruthless Positivity is everywhere these days," Dee said. "We all know it works, so anyone ignoring the formula is just being lazy, and doesn't deserve to live their very best life."

Dee might as well have programmed the moment. A beat after she finished, the wall went bright and Julia Grace was filling the very wide screen. Bright yellow letters, big as the Malt Shoppe and bright as the sun, announcing *Ruthless Positivity 2.0 — COMING SOON.*

The ad was only visual, but they could all surely hear that famous voice in their ears, chiming in time to the ticker running right under her radiant face: *We are exactly who we decide to be.*

It had been playing a lot, and Ruthless Positivity ads were always intriguing. Julia looked better than ever, but it was her son, Lyle, in the ads that everyone was always talking about.

"Dammit, he's gorgeous," Dee said.

"He's practically a prince." Raquel was still staring at Lyle's giant face as his mother's faded away.

Kam hated Ruthless Positivity, maybe more than anything else in the world. But it wasn't like she would utter an ill word about it out loud.

Kelso said, "My mom made me take the program, but I'm *so* glad I did."

"Same," Raquel and Dee said in unison.

"What about you?" Kelso turned to Kam. "When did your parents enroll you in Ruthless Positivity?"

Her friends liked to talk about the same things on repeat, because every time around was yet another chance to improve the stories they told themselves.

"Proudly for most of my life," Kam said. "Ruthless Positivity totally changed my life."

"Because you did the work," Kelso added.

Kam had been talking the talk for a while, but the clash between her words and thoughts filled her insides with vinegar. Conversations she once had to suffer through were now a breeze, so long as she followed the rules. And right now she was off the rails.

There had always been a chasm between the way Kam felt and what she was supposed to say. But it wasn't as though she could ever just turn those unspeakable thoughts off, or even lower their volume. They were always there, and occasionally deafening. The one thing she could do, and had been doing with increasing regularity as her time inside eScape assumed more purpose and import, was to go ahead and think that negative thought, whatever it might be, then neutralize it with a healing codicil immediately after. Like how her dad used to always add *between the sheets* while reading his fortune cookies out loud, and usually drunk.

Kam thought whatever she needed to think, then followed it with an old quote by Oscar Wilde in her head: *The truth is pure and rarely simple.*

She had made friends with this crew for a reason, and she couldn't forget that. Kam had wanted to be like them for her entire life. She couldn't disagree with them, not now that she was so close to getting what she really needed.

Fortunately, she didn't have to worry. Kam had been acknowledged, and now they were back to the regular self-aggrandizing merry-go-round. For now, she could look at the screen, staring dreamily at Lyle's perfect face as it faded away.

Her work would soon be finished, then Kam could live in eScape for the rest of her life. If she was right, and she could turn her world into Heaven, the rest of her life might equal forever.

Too bad there were about a million ways for her to ruin it first.

Chapter Two

Lyle

LYLE WAS ENJOYING his reprieve from hell.

eScape was his only escape, and this Malt Shoppe, appropriately enough, felt sweetest of all. He found the place a few trips ago, and had made it one of his stops ever since. He couldn't even explain why it grabbed him so hard. It wasn't just the unlimited milkshakes that touched his tongue and sat in his stomach without ever once making him feel ill, no matter how many he drank. There was something special about the air in here. Different than what he felt while outside.

His time was even more valuable inside eScape. Mother didn't know he was here, or that he was wearing a different skin. A secret avatar he could never let her discover. She would take it away, like she robbed him of everything else that he loved. Lyle could only stay away for so long. Still, it was the time for him to stop by the Shoppe, and sit for a few minutes sipping his cookies and cream.

It seemed he spent half of his life keeping every negative thought inside while chewing on his bottom lip. There was something ugly and menacing inside him, distending and begging for eScape.

But Lyle always had to swallow it, by virtue of his birthright.

The table full of self-help groupies one row over didn't have a clue about any of that. Lyle wished he could ignore their chatter, but the conversational volume was swelling instead of receding. Sometimes being famous was like a bottomless bowl of ice cream, or milkshake as it were, but most of the time it felt more like a festering sore. A blight on Lyle's life; the one thing holding him back, keeping his incessantly required smile skirting the unending edge of artifice. More often than not, it's what made him feel like dying.

You seem awfully interested in the girl with freckles on her nose. Would you like me to run a scan?

"I'm not interested in anyone," Lyle muttered to Vox, his AI assistant.

You have looked over at her table fourteen times in the last six minutes. That's more than—

"Fine. Run a scan."

Her profile is set to private.

"You couldn't have told me that ahead of time?"

I was not yet authorized to run the scan.

Lyle shook his head to himself, taking a long sip of milkshake. Vox didn't deserve the cool name that Lyle had given him. He'd named his secret avatar Jaxon, but he might as well have called his AI ASST7X419 or something equally indifferent. The assistant had about as much personality as a handful of sand. Lyle longed for an upgrade, but unlike his life in the real world, in eScape he could afford only the basics.

Lyle looked back down at his milkshake to keep

himself from looking at the pretty girl with a spray of freckles on her nose. He wanted to blame the observation on Vox, but of course Lyle had noticed her already. Every one of the fourteen times he'd looked over. Fifteen now.

Maybe his life wouldn't feel like a prison if he became famous for something *he'd* done, instead of something his mother did exactly nine months before he was born. *Lyle* had accomplished nothing, at least not anything the world would care about if he wasn't already famous for being one half of the planet's most celebrated mother and son. But that was a harness he never once asked for.

Lyle had longed to be a kid, and for as long as he could remember. Mother dangled it for more than a decade, keeping his childhood just out of his reach. One more stage, one more seminar, one more retreat for their Inner Sanctum — the most expensive one of their embarrassing number of offerings.

According to the law, Lyle had been an adult for nearly three years. He was weeks away from legally gambling if he wanted to — he didn't — and yet Mother still treated him like a child. He had no autonomy. If his life choices were limbs he would have been reduced to a torso or less already, and a long time ago.

A marionette that belonged to his mother, caught in a perpetual loop of manipulation, forced against his will (and despite his ample wealth) to sell absurdly overpriced retreats to those who could afford it, and what felt like infinitely tiered life courses for everyone else. All of it under the ambiguous yet ambitious-sounding umbrella, *Ruthlessly Positive.*

That name had always bothered Lyle. Ever since he could understand the words. *Ruthless* was negative. The two syllables together even sounded like bad news. He thought he might be wrong, since he'd been raised to think that a lot, so he checked. Three online dictionaries agreed with the printed one Mother had in her library. That volume was almost a half-century old, but fifty years hadn't changed its meaning at all. The word still meant cruel or heartless or any of the other countless synonyms implying a lack of charity.

How could they be in the business of helping people, like Mother always insisted, if they were ruthless about it? Lyle was only four years old the first time he asked her. He couldn't remember the answer, though he could imagine her rolling eyes thanks to the parade of encounters since. Lyle only knew he was four because of how often Mother had snapped at him whenever he questioned her. Telling Lyle that he had been up her ass about that since before he was five.

He had continued to inquire, and Mother had kept on feeding him reasons, everything from, *The cognitive dissonance between the two words acts as an anchor in the human brain, making it more likely that the people we're trying to help will actually be helped,* to another pair of syllables that sounded ominous, and in this instance an awful lot like the final word: *Branding.*

Eventually, Lyle stopped asking. He was around twelve or so when he finally decided that the arguments were too hard to win, especially compared to the rewards he reaped while maintaining his silence. So he shut his mouth and held it closed for the most part, hating his life but wearing a smile that everyone loved like a uniform. He kept it wide, the way the world always wanted it to be, knowing that even the slightest hint of unhappiness or display of discontent could tank the family business.

Even if Lyle could manage to forget it all, Mother would never fail to remind him.

It felt like a curse: he hated their conversations, and yet, she was the only one he could ever really talk to. At least outside in the world. And that's why he came here.

Lyle had just started visiting eScape and already its reality (artificial though it might be) felt more remarkable than he had ever allowed himself to imagine. He'd obviously been inside before, but only when wearing a leash. There was little difference between luxury resorts in the real world, and those in a digital environment. Not that he was ever allowed to explore that truth by himself.

Everything was different on his own. He couldn't afford to do much, but Lyle didn't need to. Wandering the streets and sipping a milkshake was enough. He just needed time away from his mom. He never wanted to leave the place, which was why he had to limit his experiences, and how long he was willing to stay once inside each time. He had to measure his attraction. Getting pulled in too deep would surely ruin him.

Lyle couldn't afford the discovery, but he also couldn't afford that much time inside eScape when it came down to the credits. It had taken him more than three years to pull off the small hoard of savings he had. He should've started earlier, he stayed naive enough through adolescence to believe that Mother would deliver on her promise and allow him to experience eScape for himself after turning eighteen.

But she lied about that, same as she'd led him on about so many other things. It took Lyle two years of saving his monthly allotment, with a few artificial purchases here and there so there was never too much missing at once and it was less likely to look suspicious. He needed a year to cover the startup costs, another year to cover monthly fees, upgrades, and any experiences he might want to have while inside. Plus the shithole apartment to house his secret

Nest. All those credits for special permissions and a faux persona.

Inside, Lyle Grace had nothing to do with Ruthlessly Positive, or his mother. In here he was just another twenty-year-old kid, eager to get going with the rest of his life.

He took another sip of his milkshake, still keeping his eyes away from the girl one table over. He'd been wishing for a distraction, but the walls went bright with an ad he knew all too well, and right now hated more than anything in the world. Ruthless Positivity 2.0 could go to hell and stay there.

The worst part about all of this was that Lyle had nothing to complain about. He wasn't stupid, it was easy enough to see what everyone else did. Piercing blue eyes, a mop of perfectly coifed brown hair that was treated to a weekly trim whether he wanted it or not, falling like a cartoon character's mane just below his slightly oversized eyes. Lyle was always dressed in clothes that were somehow high-fashion yet accessible, which made sense since his wardrobe choices had made it into Ruthlessly Positive's available items for sale, same as Mother's had for more than a decade.

Lyle was rich and handsome, talented and loved the world over. He didn't have the right to feel like he had any problems. Compared to most of the planet, he was a prince complaining about a pebble in his shoe. And that made Lyle feel like a heel. Woe was him, moping around about how awful his life was while living in Elysium and taking more than his share.

But here in eScape, none of that mattered.

He raised his hand, waited for a server, then ordered another milkshake — no, a sundae — once the spritely thing had skipped over to the table. Triple chocolate. Because, *why not?*

Lyle stole another glance at the table, mostly because by now it seemed like one of those puzzles where he was supposed to look at a picture and determine what about it was off.

What in this picture doesn't fit?

Of course it was the girl, sitting at the edge of the booth, both like she didn't belong and like she owned the place. Clearly comfortable in her skin, while also somehow seeming out of body. She spoke less than anyone at the table. By word count alone she was several conversations behind. But it was obvious by her eyes that she was capturing every sentence and running them all through some sort of calculations. Anyone could mask their appearance in eScape, but even in here a person's eyes didn't lie, making true intentions harder to hide.

The girl reminded him of a bird on its perch.

He had been intentionally tuning out, but now grabbing a snippet of their conversation, he wanted to tune himself back in. Three out of the four of them were wearing yoga pants and crystal jewelry, bragging about the epiphanies that Ruthlessly Positive had ushered into their lives. Only the bird on her perch remained silent.

Lyle couldn't have cared less about any of that. If he wanted to hear more, he could comb through any one of the thousands of testimonials Mother had gathered over the years. Most were real enough, since people were willing to believe whatever the hell might serve them best.

But Lyle was leaning slightly forward, as much as he could without being obvious, now that the conversation had shifted to him. And he wasn't surprised to hear that only one of the four had anything interesting to say.

Female Vapid Avatar Number One: "I bet his smallest house has more than a hundred rooms."

Male Vapid Avatar: "I bet his allowance is a million credits per month."

Female Vapid Avatar Number Two: "Who cares? Have you ever seen anyone hotter in your life?"

Male Vapid Avatar: "Of course."

And the bird on her perch said nothing.

Lyle felt himself boiling. He'd heard it all before. It happened in the real world same as in here. The difference was, no one knew who he was inside eScape, so a group of girls could be talking about Lyle Grace without having any idea that they were practically genuflecting to his face.

He hated exchanges like this because they proved his mother right. She had been feeding him a poison he didn't want to accept, yet it seemed like every eavesdropped conversation illustrated her point and made it that much harder to disbelieve. Mother insisted that women were gold diggers. It wasn't their fault, at Lyle's level of fame it would be impossible for anyone to ever see him for who he truly was. No one could ever see or hear or love him like she could.

The server set Lyle's sundae on the table. He needed something sweet to wash away all the bitterness. At least he was here, safe in his anonymity, back to eavesdropping when maybe he shouldn't be.

"We dream, we grow, we're reborn," said Female Vapid Avatar Number One.

Lyle rolled his eyes, but no one was looking at him, and it wouldn't matter if they were. The conversation grew increasingly ridiculous, with three out of four of them now quoting his mother.

Male Vapid Avatar said, "Curiosity is the driver of fulfillment."

"We're mystics of the biosphere," added Female Vapid Avatar Number Two.

Lyle was out of his seat, grabbing his shake on the way to hold as a prop.

Are you sure about this? Vox asked.

But Lyle ignored it.

"Excuse me …" he said, cutting into their conversation. "I couldn't help but overhearing. You're talking about Ruthlessly Positive, right?"

"Julia Grace is a genius," said Female Avatar Number Two.

Really, she's not.

"A lot of people like her." It was the kindest thing Lyle could say.

"That's because she's a genius," piped Female Avatar Number Two.

"Maybe you can help me," Lyle said, turning toward her with a smile. "I just don't understand what she's saying. What does *We're mystics of the biosphere* even mean?"

Half the table was already rolling their eyes.

But not the bird on her perch.

Male Vapid Avatar answered. "The complexity of the present demands an evolution of our hope if we expect for our species to survive."

"I've heard the quote, but what does it *mean?*" Lyle waited for his answer, but no one spoke. "Anyone?"

"It's hard to know where to start," said Male Vapid Avatar, not even trying.

Female Vapid Avatar Number One tried slightly harder. "Navigating the life-affirming quantum soup can be difficult if you've never experienced life at a cosmic scale."

"So how can you be expected to heal?" added Female Vapid Avatar Number Two, without actually adding anything.

"But what does any of that *mean?*" Lyle pressed. Then

into the silence he tried again, still not making eye contact with his only reason for being at their table in the first place. "You're just repeating Julia Grace quotes, but can any of you tell me what she's actually trying to say?"

It was asinine, hearing them parroting some of the most ridiculous crap from Mother's insipid workshops. The more expensive ones heaped the bullshit in mountainous piles. Her wealthiest clients were always willing to spend more to believe more.

"Sorry you're a loser who doesn't get it," said Female Vapid Avatar Number Two.

"Yearning is born in the gap where coherence has been excluded. Yes, it is possible to obliterate the things that confront us, but not without will on our side. While there is ego, learning cannot thrive," Lyle replied, in his best impression of Mother.

The table didn't know what to do with that. Their expressions were frozen, smug yet paralyzed, wanting him to understand how much further evolved they were than him. And sure, a part of Lyle took perverse satisfaction in the irony, picturing their mortified horror if they only knew who they were actually talking to. That same part of him wanted to reveal himself to make them realize just how stupid they were.

But his short-lived satisfaction would be replaced with immediate regret once word got out that he was in here, once word got to Mother. And then his entire purpose for escaping into this world and its anonymity would be gone.

They all regarded him with such condescension. Except for the bird, still on her perch, looking up at him with eyes that were so different than the rest of them. Without even opening her mouth she had already said so much.

Lyle kept hoping she would break the stalemate and speak to him.

Instead she kept her lips on the straw.

"Any thoughts?"

They all stared at him blankly, except the bird who kept observing him in seeming interest.

"That's what I thought," Lyle said, turning around and marching outside the Shoppe.

We're going to The Palisades, aren't we?

"Of course we're going to The Palisades," Lyle growled.

Yet another unforgettable virtual adventure that he wouldn't be able to enjoy, but felt like he had to experience, just to forget the discomfort, or at least leave it behind. Something that cost a fraction here of what it would in the real world where Lyle had probably experienced whatever it was already.

He longed for something true. A place where he could really be himself, and someone to be himself with. A world where he wouldn't have to feign perfection, or that he was someone else, a place where he wouldn't have to act happy when there was a gnarled ball of unrest, knotted and rotten inside him.

At least in eScape he could pretend to be someone else, but that didn't mean Lyle would ever be able to find someone to love him for who he was, not if he could never be himself.

The thought was driving him crazy, and right now there was only one thing Lyle could do to get it out of his head.

And that's exactly what he had to do.

. . .

LYLE STEPPED out of the hot air balloon and onto the grass, wishing he felt better than he had before the ride. But he didn't. The Palisades were supposed to provide an eScape, but right now he still felt empty enough to edge hopeless. It was bad enough feeling that way in the real world, here in this digital wonderland, such negative emotions should have been extinct.

He should forget about feeling anything good for now. Lyle was overdue to get home. He looked behind him at the assembly of balloons and wondered if he was broken for good. The Palisades offered unparalleled adventure, and yet Lyle was apparently incapable of enjoying any of them.

He was back from Turkey, though he'd never really gone. He wanted an unforgettable experience, but despite the full immersion, Lyle couldn't keep himself from remembering that it was all artificial.

Cappadocia was stunning. One of the most peculiar-looking places on Earth, with odd formations called fairy chimneys jutting up a hundred feet into the sky, and ancient underground cities below the surface. Lyle's balloon took off at first light, or what passed for it in that part of the simulation. As the sun rose, a lunar landscape slowly peeled back from the planet to reveal a cardinal-colored sky. It should have taken his breath away, but it didn't.

Instead of basking in the beauty, Lyle kept thinking about that perched bird from the Malt Shoppe, even though he didn't want to. Picturing her was fine, but the image always accompanied Mother's voice, reminding her son that there was only one reason anyone would ever want to be with him. Now back on the ground, Lyle thought he might be seeing things. There she was, rounding the corner and coming his way, holding what looked like one of those specialty coffees from The Screaming Beans Cafe.

Lyle replayed their exchange from the Malt Shoppe, wondering if he'd said anything to give himself away, knowing that he shouldn't have even gone over there. He could prove Mother wrong in the real world, but he needed to stay invisible while inside eScape.

She stopped in front of him, meeting his gaze with her gold-digging eyes.

"Why are you following me?" Lyle asked.

"I'm not." Her spray of freckles scrunching together, appearing surprised by the question.

"You were at the Malt Shoppe, and now you're here."

"I followed you. That doesn't mean I'm *following you.*"

Now she was playing word games. "So you followed me here, then waited around until I finished."

She held up her cup. "I wanted a coffee."

"After already drinking a shake?"

"We're in eScape." She shrugged.

"Why did you follow me?" And now he was letting his impatience show.

"I wanted to talk."

"We already talked," Lyle said.

She shook her head. "*You* talked, and so did my friends. But in case you didn't notice, I was only listening."

He had noticed. "So, was there something you wanted to say, now that you've had all this time to think about it?"

"Just that I agree with you … about those Julia Grace quotes being bullshit." She gave him a tiny smile. "And I also wanted to compliment your impression of her. It's seriously the best one I've ever heard."

He'd had a lifetime of practice. "Do you hear a lot of Julia Grace impressions?"

"No, but yours was still great." She laughed and held out her hand. "I'm Kam."

Lyle took it, surprised by how much he actually wanted to. "I'm Jaxon."

"Well, it's great to meet you, Jaxon." A beat, then, "Is that your real name, or something you only use inside eScape?"

It was a simple question, plenty of people had legal aliases in this place, but Lyle was hiding for a specific reason and couldn't afford to unveil himself. Their conversation felt suddenly dangerous. Sure, it would be great to engage with someone who hadn't bought into Mother's bullshit, but he had to be careful. It had taken him years to finally get here.

"It's my real name," Lyle lied.

Kam nodded, seemingly satisfied. "So, why do you have a problem with Julia Grace?"

"I never said I had a problem with her." At least not out loud.

"Well then, maybe it's a problem with Ruthless Positivity, but you came over to our table. And I understand how it is when you can't keep an opinion to yourself: there's *always a reason*. So tell me, Jaxon, what's your beef with Julia Grace?"

She smiled, awaiting his answer.

"Because it's pseudoscience psychobabble."

Kam nodded. "Sounds about right."

"Do *you* have a problem with Ruthless Positivity, too? Or are you just curious about mine?"

"I have plenty of issues with Julia Grace" — the girl spit her name like a curse — "*and* Ruthless Positivity."

"Like?" Lyle prompted.

"Like my father basically raised me with that crap. Ruthless Positivity was his religion. He shoveled that shit

22

into my brain, from long before I could think for myself until well after I was old enough to question everything."

"I'm sorry to hear that." And really, he was. "Where is your father now?"

Kam looked at the ground, moving her coffee from one hand to the other before looking back up and into his eyes. "He's dead."

A beat of embarrassment before Lyle found his two-word answer. "I'm sorry."

She shrugged. "It happened a while ago."

"How?" Lyle dared. Then to soften his curiosity he added, "Was it sudden?"

"Yes and no." She took a breath. "My father was schizophrenic, but wasn't so great about taking his meds. Things were already wrong with his brain, but they got a lot worse after my mom died. I was five years old and Dad was … having a hard time."

She needed another breath. Then Kam continued with the thinnest of smiles. "He went to a Ruthlessly Positive parenting seminar, and apparently had some sort of religious experience. He left the convention feeling like God was punishing me for being such a wild child by taking his wife away from him. Not my mother," she clarified, "*his wife.*"

Lyle hoped his face didn't show his horror. "Were you … a wild child, I mean?"

"Not in the slightest." She shook her head. "But he latched onto the program anyway. Dad was obsessed with Julia Grace and made me attend my first seminar a year later."

"And how was that?" Lyle felt momentarily hopeful. Bullshit or not, attendees usually left their seminars with a renewed outlook and the will to be better. Ruthlessly so.

"Terrible," Kam answered, her voice gaining weight.

"He latched onto the program and basically used Ruthlessly Positive's pop psychology to punitively raise me."

He didn't need to hear further explanation. Lyle had to live with her, and was well-versed in how easy it had always been for his mom to ruin someone's life.

"When did he die?"

"When I was fifteen. His schizophrenia peaked. His behavior became extremely erratic, and the hallucinations were a *lot* more frequent."

"Hallucinations?"

"Oh yeah. He saw shit all the time. It was exhausting, always trying to take care of him, while also taking care of myself." She stopped again, this time with something he felt sure Kam wasn't saying. But then she reset herself and finished. "One day he left the house in the middle of seeing something that wasn't really there, and I made the mistake of not trying to stop him."

"What happened?" Lyle felt guilty for asking, but he was still learning forward.

"He stepped in front of a bus and was killed instantly."

"So it was suicide?"

"No." She shook her head. "He probably saw a dragon or a demon or some other monster instead of the bus. Probably thought he could kill it with his bare fists or something."

"Shit …"

"Yeah," Kam agreed. "*Shit.*"

The following seconds were both silent and strange. Lyle felt somehow plugged into this girl, and that was a new experience. This moment of connection with a stranger — it was exactly what attendees claimed to experience at Ruthlessly Positive seminars all the time.

"You must be so angry," he finally said.

Lyle thought he understood how she felt, but Kam surprised him again. "I'm not angry at all."

"You're not?"

Another shake of her head, followed by yet another shrug. "I just feel numb, like the whole thing happened to someone else. Someone who doesn't even matter anymore."

"Oh." Lyle was still feeling surprised, this time by an unexpected emotion. Jealousy, or something dangerously close. This girl had suffered something awful, maybe even worse than what he had been living through, and yet she had found it in herself to somehow forgive the father who ruined her life.

But he couldn't do that. Lyle loathed his own father, and that wasn't something that could ever change. The asshole had abandoned them when Lyle was two: ground zero for everything else that had ever gone wrong in his life. Like the love-hate relationship he had with his mother, who constantly used the idea that her son was the "man of the house" as a two-handed weapon, constantly treating Lyle like a substitute for her missing husband. Manipulating him through an incessant blending of feigned helplessness, guilt-tripping and shaming him for being "just like his father" whenever he refused to do as she wished, or had the gall to question her.

Mother eventually tracked his father down, only to discover that he was working as a bartender, no longer a psychiatrist. The loser had left a steady string of one-night stands and gambling losses behind him, living his life beneath an umbrella of general misbehavior, proving to the world that no woman would ever boss him around again. Lyle had spent his adolescence disgusted by his dad, but also more envious than he cared or dared to admit. In truth, his father was free, and the older Lyle got, the more he craved that freedom for himself.

Kam was still looking at him, waiting for him to respond with something other than, *Oh.*

But what *could* he say? Lyle was sympathetic. Even if it wasn't criminal for Mother to sell seminars when someone needed medical treatment instead, it should be. Despite knowing how much blather there was in her message, Lyle never considered the depth of harm her system might be causing. He had seen all the smiles, and for the most part believed in the placebo effect Mother insisted that everyone was getting, "at the very least."

"What do *you* believe?" Kam asked, finally breaking the silence.

"I'm sorry?"

"You felt strongly enough about Ruthlessly Positive to come over, so what's the story there?"

Lyle had too many replies and not a clue where to start. He opened his mouth, then immediately closed it. Clenched his fist and flexed his fingers, wondering what he could say.

Right or wrong, glittering gold or pieces of iron pyrite, Ruthlessly Positive was his family business and Lyle could never forget it. If he couldn't be positive, and ruthlessly so, then maybe he didn't even deserve the air he was breathing or the breath in his lungs, or so said an oft-quoted Julia Grace.

"I don't have an opinion about the program one way or the other," he lied. "I only came over because it seemed like no one at your table had any idea what they were talking about. Except you, of course."

"I don't believe you," she said, with an alluring shake of her head. "What aren't you saying?

Clench and unclench. "Nothing, really. I mean, sure, I

have my doubts about some of it, but the program has apparently helped a ton of people, so it can't *all* be bad, can it?"

"You might not feel that way if you grew up with it shoved down your throat," she argued.

But Lyle couldn't argue back. "Do you want to go inside The Palisades?"

Surprise found her face like a ray of morning sun. It took her seconds to respond. In that pause she appeared to process disbelief. "Didn't you just get out of there?"

"Yep."

"Those trips are expensive; why go again?"

"Last time I went alone. And no worries, I'll pay for you."

"I can pay for myself," Kam said, already walking back toward The Palisades, fast.

He fell in step beside her, and was pleased to catch the edge of a smile. It was contagious. Lyle found himself with one of his own as he realized that he hadn't walked in step with anyone inside eScape. He came here looking to flee loneliness, but it always found him anyway. Kam wasn't exactly his friend, but it felt like she might be the start of something.

"So, how does it work?" she asked, a few long strides from The Palisades.

"You've never been?"

"I prefer real experiences."

"None of this is real," Lyle said.

"Guess we use the word differently." Her smile hadn't gone anywhere. She tipped her chin up to a large marquee and repeated her question. "So, how does it work?"

Lyle followed her eyes to the marquee. "We pick the experience and pay. Simple as that."

"Which ones have you done?" Kam asked, her eyes still on the marquee.

"A bunch of them. Today I did Cappadocia."

Her gaze found Turkey and she nodded with approval. "Which ones *haven't* you done? Or better yet, which of those would you try if I wasn't here with you?"

"Why not ask me about the best one I've been on, so that way you'll know it's good?"

"I assume they're all good. Otherwise they couldn't charge so much. And I'd rather we're both going in virgins so you don't know anything more than me."

Lyle laughed and she laughed along with him.

"Fair enough. How about Nakasendo Way?"

She scanned the description, then turned back to Lyle. "No way."

"Why not? Everyone's seen Tokyo, rural Japan is way more impressive."

"I've never seen Tokyo, and Nakasendo Way is a five-day walk."

"You can leave whenever you want to."

"Then what's the point, doing it only partway?" Now she looked bothered, shaking her head. "And besides, we just met, I'm not hiking with you for five days."

Lyle only wanted to see what she would say. He was overdue to log out himself. He raised his hands in surrender. "Fine. How about Easter Island?"

She liked that, he could see it in her eyes. "How long will that take?"

"However long you want it to."

"I only have an hour."

"And then you turn into a pumpkin?"

"I have an hour, Jaxon. Will that be a problem?" Her eyes were as stern as her voice.

"Not a problem at all." And still his smile was easy to find.

THEY WERE on the island a lot longer than an hour, and before she started flipping out, Lyle was wondering how he would ever explain such a long absence to Mother. He'd been gone long enough that for sure he would have questions to answer. But still, trading his posh home for a few hours in the shithole apartment so he could access eScape was like water in the desert.

It changed everything, having someone there to enjoy The Palisades alongside him. In the real world they were in two different places living two entirely different lives. But here in eScape, Lyle and Kam were walking side-by-side hundreds of miles off the coast of Mainland Chile. Rapa Nui if you lived there. Not that any of the AI citizens of this version of Easter Island did.

They kept talking and talking and talking some more while walking the beaches and observing the Moai statues. Lyle suggested cresting a rise and looking at the wild horses supposedly running on the other side, but that's when Kam started losing it.

She had to go, *now*. It really was like Cinderella after midnight. Her body language changed, becoming suddenly frantic. She seemed almost angry.

"Bad news is, time flies," he said, trying to soothe her. "Good news is, you're the pilot."

That seemed to make things worse. They left The Palisades fast, with him apologizing the entire time. He obviously said something to upset her, Lyle just didn't know what. Once past the gates he planned to apologize a final time before asking Kam when he could see her again.

But the words never left his mouth.

Outside The Palisades, Kam was already gone, first turning into a Cheshire Cat, before fading away, leaving only a smile, followed by nothing.

Lyle stared at the empty space where Kam had been standing just seconds before. There weren't any words for the way he was feeling, full and empty in unison.

He had to find her again.

After he lied to Mother.

Chapter Three

Kam

Kam was back at the Malt Shoppe, alone this time.

Maybe she should have picked a different place. Kam could disappear the second she saw someone. But still, she felt exposed. Not much of a choice, really, the Malt Shoppe was the one place in eScape where she felt most at home. The best place to sit with a liquid dessert she couldn't enjoy in real life, ruminating about her conversation with Jaxon, who, after slurping the bottom of her third shake, she was feeling ever more certain might maybe *possibly* be Lyle Grace himself.

As the cliché went, it wasn't what he said, it was how he said it.

Bad news is, time flies. Good news is, you're the pilot.

Kam had heard the Prince of Positivity say that same thing more times than she could count, and for more than half of her life. The words were identical, but so was his inflection. And in the moment, it sure didn't seem like Jaxon had been making a joke. He said it like Lyle would have while trying to convince an audience that time was on their side when it obviously wasn't.

It didn't seem possible that Kam had really been talking to Lyle all that time, but her hard-working heart and craving for yet another milkshake wanted to argue that she was.

She took out her phone and scrolled through pages of videos until she found the one she was looking for. Before the video started, an obnoxious advertisement showed the benefits of having a LifePod, a portable house that allowed you to never leave the comforts of home while on the road. The ad featured none other than Julia and Kyle, sitting cozily next to one another. Lyle even did a thumbs-up as he said, "And it even has a Nest!"

Ugh. Something is wrong when even the rich people's portable houses are a hundred times nicer than mine.

She hit the *Skip Ad* button the minute she was able as the video began — a compilation of Lyle Grace saying those words over and over, in a variety of scenarios:

Bad news is, time flies. Good news is, you're the pilot.
Bad news is, time flies. Good news is, you're the pilot.
Bad news is, time flies. Good news is, you're the pilot.

Exactly the same, every time. Just like when she heard it as they scurried out of The Palisades together. Jaxon's face looked little like Lyle's, but it didn't have to. Not inside eScape. Anyone would be horrified to see how very different she was.

Kam stopped the video, swiped away from her Lyle Grace playlist, and started back through the many files she had gathered over the years. She'd never really been able to get him fully out of her head. A childhood crush was embarrassing enough, a lifelong obsession was infinitely worse. What the hell was wrong with her?

The truth wasn't nearly as bad as it looked, but how

could Kam ever really explain things? She had so many files on Lyle because whether he knew it or not he'd been an important part of her life. But that's all they were, *files*. She didn't have a murder board or a crazy shrine, and was following his life with curiosity and care, without ever having made a single plan to stalk him.

Kam never imagined that she'd run into him inside eScape. *If* that's what had actually happened. Right now, it was impossible to know, and Kam wondered if she would ever find out.

A tickle at her throat. It was suddenly hard to breathe. She tried to inhale but it was like trying to suck tar through her nose. She choked and coughed, then reset her brain, finally remembering the release valve that had gone unturned for too long.

The turmoil wasn't unexpected. Kam was used to the constant inner debate.

She thought the words: *The truth is pure and rarely simple.*

Then, to make sure her mind knew this was serious, she said them out loud in a whisper. "The truth is pure and rarely simple."

And again she could breathe.

But that didn't mean she was finished hating herself.

Kam knew exactly who she was. And it wasn't the spritely girl sitting at the Malt Shoppe, gulping three shakes in a row, or the one trying to hold her own with this sector's Reginas. Yes, she was both of those girls, and outside eScape Kam still had freckles on her nose. But she was also a 23-year-old invalid suffering from a degenerative disease who had withered most of her life away in bed, buried in tutorials and practical application, learning to program, then pushing her knowledge uphill as hard as she could during every hour she didn't spend sleeping. Of those there were few.

She'd had a singular goal: to hack her way into eScape. Inside she could see what life might be like outside of her prison, if she could live instead of visit. Enter more as a citizen than as a tourist. But she could barely afford the AI assist, and her avatar would have nothing. Everything cost credits, same as in the real world. The scale was different, closer to infinite within eScape, but there was an entirely separate economy living just under the real one.

Kam needed to enter rich, and stay invisible. At first she'd been looking for a big score, with a large enough haul to feed her forever. But then she saw the flaw in that logic. If Kam wanted to score a million credits, it made a lot more sense to skim a thousand each from people who would never even notice they were gone, than work for a jackpot that would draw unwanted attention.

If someone was willing to spend twenty thousand credits on their wardrobe just so they would have something new on their skin whenever they went online, Kam saw them as fair game. She was a natural at lifting what she needed, a hundred here, a thousand there. Once, Kam skimmed six figures from some asshole who kept going to The Silk, a sector of eScape no one talked about, and pretended didn't exist. Whatever he was doing there, he could pay an extra hundred thousand credits for it. Kam didn't even care if she got caught, until the worry wormed inside her and then refused to leave.

Hacking was life in prison, no questions asked. Kam was already serving that sentence in her own way, so it didn't feel like much of a threat. But still, she'd learned more than how to steal. She was still surprising herself with the things she was learning to do. Kam might be one of the best hackers in the world. It was hard to know, since her breed stayed invisible. But being the best didn't matter to her. She was a lot better than plenty good enough for what she needed, and better than that considering her recent ambitions. What shouldn't be possible, but maybe was.

Maybe.

Kam occasionally waded her way through a wave of guilt, seeing herself as a thief. But then she would hear someone referring to the base-level users as lessers and forget her morals. It wasn't like she was stealing real credits that people needed to live. Kam kept her earnings in eScape while every day life took more than it gave her back. She was twenty-three, and even if she had unlimited wealth and five-star healthcare, Kam would be lucky to see her thirtieth birthday. Soon the years would turn even more pallid, jaundiced of awareness, doped up on opiates to dim her pain into less of a menace.

It wasn't worth it. Kam knew what she wanted. Why should she have to suffer in a broken body for a few extra years when she could (theoretically) live forever, young and healthy, from within an incandescent eternity? Life was hard, but eScape was uncomplicated and vacant of pain. One was a burning candle, the other a pile of ash.

Inside, Kam owned a Malt Shoppe and could have as many shakes as she wanted. Outside, she hadn't ordered dessert in years. Even if she was willing to spend the credits on her tastebuds instead of yet another tool for her hacking, she would vomit it all before finishing.

Inside Kam could go wherever she wanted, and buy or do whatever she wanted. Outside she lived on a dole that was barely enough to keep her breathing, and couldn't do anything more than ignore the degenerative disease that was slowly killing her. *Autumn Bronchitis*, an idiotic nickname for a new sickness that ravaged the planet Earth in the early 20s. Kam was born with it in utero; she never stood a chance.

Kam used to be able to do things like walk to the corner store or clean her house. Now she was completely dependent on her neighbor. That might not be so bad, if Lucinda wasn't born again and wasting an embarrassing number of breaths always trying to save her. She needed help with the groceries, not her eternal soul. On the surface, Lucinda was a sweetheart, but under her big pink heart she was a religious nut who got off on treating Kam like some sort of personal charity case. It could be worse, she could still be getting "help" from Jeremiah.

He seemed nice at first, but by his third visit Kam saw Jeremiah for the monster he was. Due to her condition, she was eligible for a visit once each week from a state-paid care worker trained in empathy. But it was hard to take his fellowship seriously when he told Kam to "put her mouth on it." It wasn't even a request; the order was growled and sounded involuntary, the way it rolled right out of his jowls. Jeremiah kept yelling apologies while Kam buried herself behind a locked bathroom door, staying inside on the floor for a full fifteen minutes after she was sure and a half that he'd left.

Sometimes Kam fantasized about hacking that pile of shit and ruining his life, but that was a negative emotion that felt cancerous inside her. She didn't agree with the ruthless part of Ruthless Positivity, but she did believe in nixing the negativity, and managed to make it true for herself more often than not.

There were better things to fantasize about, so Kam kept her daydreams aimed in only one of two directions. Either how much she could work her way up inside eScape, or maybe one day meeting Lyle Grace as this much better version of her. Not that she ever really had any hope of that.

But she finally (probably) had, and Kam wasn't sure if

she felt more dismayed or elated. She had imagined meeting him enough times to get her blushing. She pictured them together, confessing their doubts and assumptions. In some of her fantasies Lyle told Kam that she was right — he was trapped and had been living in a hell of his own that wasn't all that different from the one that had been singeing her soul for most of a rotten lifetime by now. In other dreams he denied it at first, but even then Kam still managed to convince him in the end, getting Lyle to eventually see the crystal clear truth that Ruthless Positivity was a wicked iniquitous lie.

He was logging into eScape as someone else. On a whiteboard that didn't make sense, but Kam could see beyond the obvious. She knew who Lyle was, who he had always been, and who he would be if she could find a way to help him.

If only she'd seen the truth sooner, assuming that's what she was seeing now. They could have had a genuine conversation. It went bad in part because Kam hadn't known who she was talking to, but Lyle was so different from what she expected that it wouldn't have made any difference anyway. She couldn't stop herself, blathering on and on and on about her childhood and her father and how he fucked up by draining their savings to nothing, squandering their every dime on seminars and courses, empty promises made by Ruthless Positivity.

Kam expected an argument at the very least, but it was nothing like that. If Jaxon No Last Name Given was really Lyle Grace in the digital flesh, then he didn't waste so much as a minute of their time trying to defend his mother. He listened instead, and she wasn't used to that. Even while surrounded by her so-called friends within eScape, no one ever really wanted to hear what Kam had to say. They were only waiting for their turn to talk, or for yet another chance to crow about how much better off they had it than the rest of the world.

Mostly, Kam regretted how fast she needed to disappear, and that her departure had been so abrupt. But she didn't have a choice; Kam had to get out of there before her Deep Spell expired.

She was always stretching her body beyond what it could comfortably do, both inside and outside, but Kam had still never taken it this far. Today she'd been downright reckless, and if she wasn't careful that would destroy her. There was a reason she lived her life with so many rules, starting with the length of her visits. Deep Spells were dangerous. Not quite illegal, they were highly discouraged, and in no way intended for people like Kam, whose frail bodies were ravaged by the requirements.

Imagining herself outsmarting the system, and finding a way to leave her broken body behind in exchange for a virtual one that worked and unlimited potential, in a place with a blue sky that could actually mean something — that was how Kam put herself to sleep every night.

But she had pushed things too far during her last visit. Deep Spells were harder on her body than most, probably more so for her than anyone she knew. Kam kept her visits short, but was having such an amazing time with Jaxon — or *Lyle*, her mind kept wanting to insist — that she stayed until the pain was screaming so loud she had to leave eScape with only a Cheshire smile to remember her by.

She didn't even have a chance to ask Jaxon/Lyle if they could see each other again.

Yet, despite her blathering, Lyle had listened. And that had felt … maybe better than anything Kam had ever experienced in her life. She had been thinking hard on it for a while, and couldn't remember another time in her entire life when someone had actually listened to what she had to say, without waiting for her to hurry up and finish, or telling her she was wrong to feel what she did, or to say it out loud.

Kam kept trying to replay parts of the conversation in her head, working over the worst of what she might or might not have said. It was hard to remember with clarity, because despite a jumble of exchanges it was difficult to sift between what she articulated out loud and what she only thought. The division was usually clear, but today she barely had a filter.

What if she had offended him?

What if she ruined everything?

What if Kam ran into him again, only to find that he wanted nothing to do with her?

She had said too many things to offend him. Sure, he was arguing with her friends about Ruthless Positivity, so he clearly had issues like she'd always thought he might. But it was still his family (again, assuming he was really Lyle) and she might have gone too far.

She should have kept some of the truth to herself. How humiliating, admitting that her father had spent all of their credits. And inconsistent, seeing as how she still apparently had plenty to spend at The Palisades. Now she would have to make up a story about how she made her money, so he didn't think — *or know* — she was poor. So he didn't suspect her criminal activity that afforded her her paradise lifestyle.

She had seen something special in Lyle Grace from the back of the room for years. Dad took her, every time an RP seminar came to the Intuit Dome. From the first time she saw him, it felt like he was the only person in the world who could ever truly understand her. A fellow prisoner, even if he lived in a gilded cage.

She'd been stalking him online ever since, watching

him grow up both alongside her and at a distance. At first Kam saw him as a slightly younger little brother, and justi-fied her stalking as watching over him in a protective way. But adolescence hit hard on both sides. Lyle grew into a great-looking guy, deepening her attraction into something as biological as it was emotional.

Kam wished she could get their encounter out of her head, at least long enough to stop second-guessing herself into what felt like an emotional grave. She couldn't decide if things had gone well or terribly between them. The wondering felt like a nail in her skull.

But at least now she knew his secret identity.

Maybe Kam could engineer another chance to meet him? Remind Lyle of the times they had met before, not that he would ever remember passing her by. Let him know that she could sense his discontent. Promise what no one else probably ever had by making sure he understood that she felt the same things he did. And that he always had.

Yes, Kam would figure out exactly how to pull it off. Find Lyle, make sure their next encounter was the dream come true it could be, and maybe have a shot at the happily ever after she'd always yearned for yet never believed could really belong to her.

She grabbed her milkshake, leapt up from the booth, and made a beeline for the door.

In too much of a hurry and not paying nearly as much attention as she needed to, Kam collided with someone entering the Malt Shoppe just as she was trying to leave.

Her milkshake painted them both.

She expected fury and yelling, but instead the assaulted man fell out the door and back into the street with a surprised laugh.

Kam wanted to crawl away. She couldn't believe it. Six seconds ago she was determined to do better the next time. But here she was, crashing into Jaxon or Lyle, or whoever he was, and still she couldn't help messing everything up.

Jaxon smiled, wiping a hand down his shirt to make the milkshake disappear. And just like that, his clothes were good as new. It was the simplest of avatar upgrades, but Kam still wouldn't have been able to afford it without her vault of stolen credits.

Kam did the same, and the milkshake vanished, but the stain immediately reappeared. She tried again, but the stubborn stain remained. Her autoclean upgrade wasn't working. She looked up at Jaxon in frustration.

"It's no big deal," he said.

"Do you have any idea how much money I've made as a programming engineer?"

He shook his head, his smile receding. "No, I don't. But maybe—"

"You should see my apartment in the real world. It's almost embarrassing how much space I have. Plus a private chef and … what? What is it?"

Kam didn't like the way he was looking at her, nothing like he had been before.

She wanted to say something to reset the mood. But he'd retreated a full step away from her. Even if she wasn't her best self right now, Kam was aware enough to know this wasn't the right time.

He straightened his posture.

She shuddered with shame-ridden chills.

Kam knew this look because she'd seen it so many times before. His smile was still there, but even wearing a digital mask, he couldn't hide behind the artifice. With his seminar bearing she could see it even more clearly than before.

Jaxon was Lyle Grace.

"I'm glad that you're doing so well and I wish you the best, but I really need to be going now."

"No, please, Lyle." She swallowed. "I know who you really are."

He flinched. But there wasn't so much as a chip in his plastered smile. "It was wonderful getting to know you yesterday, but I've come to eScape for downtime and I hope you can respect my privacy."

"Of course—"

"I could get a new avatar, but that's an expensive and time-consuming legal process."

"I would never tell." Her heart was pounding, this was all going so terribly wrong.

"Keep my secret and I'll owe you a favor. Anything that's in my power to grant."

In my power to grant? Why was he talking like that? She didn't want or need to be bribed. Of course she would keep his secret.

"I would never tell." Then she blurted, "Wanna go to The Palisades together?"

"No, thank you." Lyle fell another tentative step back, trying to slip away without Kam causing a scene or blowing his cover.

"I would never want to cause you any trouble!"

I've been following you for most of your life to make sure you're okay!

Lyle looked at her with uncertainty in his eyes, along-side another emotion she couldn't decipher. It was heart-breaking, how wrong this was all going. He gave her a curt nod, then turned without another word and left her in the shadows.

She didn't understand what had happened. Not really.

Maybe Lyle didn't believe her, about the apartment

and the chef. Maybe he knew she was lying, in which case, maybe she also deserved his disgust or indifference.

But it wasn't like she could tell him the truth, that she was desperately poor. In his mind, without days of explaining behind it, she would be a thief. Only a rich person could afford her level of access.

Kam was already worried enough that she would never be able to make things right between them, she sure as hell didn't want to worry that Lyle might report his suspicions and draw attention to her before she managed to cover her tracks.

Except the Lyle she knew would never do that.

And yet, she couldn't stop questioning herself.

Because in truth, Kam wondered if maybe she didn't really know him at all. And now she might never have the chance.

Chapter Four

Kam

PEOPLE WHO SAY they love being alone probably don't have much of a choice.

Lyle abandoned Kam, leaving her with the person she loathed most. *Sometimes* she felt proud of herself, but only thanks to her level of hacking. Even that didn't make her better than anyone else; it only proved how much harder she was willing to work than a general population raised on the digital delivery of an omnipresent escape hatch from life.

But in times like these, after so thoroughly blowing it, Kam had a hard time seeing herself as anything better than the mess that she was. Wallowing was never her thing, but she could sometimes slip and fall right into it when careless. Luxuriating in misfortune would make things too easy.

Now Kam felt crushed under the unexpected weight of Lyle's rejection. It was one thing to pine from afar and dream that things might go her way once they were face-to-face, ridiculous as that fantasy might be. But she'd been given her moment and it might as well have been a line of pee down her leg for all it was worth.

Kam had to end her ruminating after a day, smelling the threat of sticking around in her sorrow too long. Getting on with it, she invited her friends over to the opulent, yet casually, furnished flat she kept above the Shoppe. She owned the entire building and had plenty of credits to decorate, or occasionally burn if she wanted to. Kam had practically copied and pasted interiors from eScape's "best of" lists while exploring the looks she might want to borrow.

Kam shoved her emotions down. Sadness, the pain of rejection, and the unrequited love did nothing to help her. So she locked it all up and tried to enjoy the company of her friends as she sat on an oversized sofa with them. They were watching Lyle's latest webinar, some stupidly named summit, replaying on her apartment's wall-sized screen. Dee's idea.

Ruthlessly Positive had an even glitzier feeling online. Julia Grace always had an eye for making everything look just so, or at least her art department did. But none of Kam's friends were interested in seeing her; they all got enough of her in the real world. Lyle's appearances were far more rare, especially recently. This was a surprise announcement, without Julia and totally out of the blue. The chance to see Lyle all on his own had filled her with hope; maybe he would show that other side of himself, the side that she suspected he kept hidden.

But Kam wasn't enjoying the summit nearly as much as her friends. Every minute kept hurting her stomach worse. *How to Manifest Love by Eliminating Your Negative Nature.* The words were all bullshit, same as everything having to do with Ruthlessly Positive. And still, Kam couldn't stand the thought of missing a syllable, for fear she'd lose out on something between the lines, and maybe meant just for her.

"It's a five-step process," Lyle continued talking down to them as they all leaned forward as one. "The first step is the most important, and for some of you it will also be the hardest."

Lyle paused, took a breath, and looked meaningfully at the camera. She'd always thought he seemed rehearsed despite his effort to appear natural, but now after meeting him in person Kam knew it like the feel of her fingernails digging crescents into her flesh.

"The first step is to *be aware*. Negativity is the offspring of fear, and you can't put your personal terror into its place without being aware of your very worst thoughts."

"He's right," Kelso nodded vigorously, "I always want to know what I'm thinking."

Dee and Raquel joined his nodding while Kam pressed her back against the cushions, watching the scene from behind everyone else on the sofa.

Lyle continued. "Only after becoming aware will you have the power to transform your situation—"

Transform your situation. It broke her heart to hear the puppeteering.

"—The more you practice being aware of your thoughts, the more you can learn to control them. And remember, you must be *ruthless*."

Another smile for the camera and another stab at her heart.

"You cannot allow that negative thought to win. No sir," Lyle shook his head, "you must reclaim your power. Stop focusing on what you don't want and start focusing on your goals instead."

"Screw the negativity!" Dee shouted at the wall.

"And screw me while you're at it!" Raquel cried out with a laugh.

"Whether you're aware of it or not, focusing on the things you don't want just puts them front and center in your mind. That upset feeling you have in your stomach …" He stared into the camera. "Where do you think that's coming from?"

Kam knew exactly where hers was coming from.

Raquel laughed. "It's because you haven't screwed me yet."

Still looking into the camera, Lyle answered his own question. "It's coming from you. So stop it. Start manifesting instead. That's the third step: demanding what you want from the Cosmos of Totality. Ask yourself: *What do I really want?* I promise: it's like having a magic wand. The moment you can shift your focus from what you don't want to what you do want, the negativity in your life will start to subside."

Kelso said, "I stopped saying that I didn't want to get fat, and started telling myself I was going to be lean for the rest of my life. Now I barely ever eat anything outside eScape."

"Totally," Dee agreed.

"The next step is easy." And Lyle's breezy voice made believing a cinch. "Change your frequency. When you're in touch with your true self, the rest is easy."

He had nothing to offer the end of that sentence beyond his smile.

But it was enough for everyone else in the room. Even Kelso seemed to be swooning.

"You change your focus to change the way you feel, then change the way you feel to change your frequency. One change precipitates the next, over and over until your fully watered garden can finally bloom."

Lyle stared into the camera as Kam swallowed her vomit.

She could hear his mother behind every word. Her hand was practically up his ass pulling the strings of her golden puppet.

Syllables festered, making her sick.

Lyle kept going, but Kam had to tune him out. They all knew every word. There was no reason for her to be watching this. It was genital-free masturbation. They might as well have been at a concert, throwing panties on stage from the front row, Kelso included. He wasn't gay, at least he'd never said as much and Kam didn't think so, but she thought he had a thing for Lyle anyway. Everyone did. The broadcast didn't just show the star from his home studio, a row of rotating boxes ran like a ticker beneath the primary window: reaction shots from throughout eScape, small crowds gathered to watch his live show. Screaming fans, mostly women.

Kelso said, "He's like the most evolved person I've ever seen in my life. I mean, his mom too, totally, but she's old. Lyle is like our age and he could totally run for president."

"I bet he will one day." Dee offered them all a knowing nod.

"I should probably screw him before then." Raquel turned to Kam. "You're awfully quiet. Are you wondering what Lyle's tongue would feel like on your—"

"No, I absolutely am not." Kam wished she could melt into the couch. Everyone was looking, wanting her to say something. "I'm just thinking."

"About what his tongue would feel like on your—"

"Leave her alone, Raquel," Dee said. "Besides, she can't cheat on Chad."

Raquel teased, "You mean the mystery boyfriend who never comes here?"

"He's busy," Kam said, a bit too defensively.

"Yeah, I think you're just afraid to share him."

Kam laughed it off. Tried to, anyway.

"Be quiet," Kelso whined. "I can't hear what he's saying."

Everyone had stopped looking, so Kam dared to roll her eyes. "You already know what he's going to say."

Kelso shook his head without turning from the wall. "That's not the point."

"Which of the Ruthless Positivity Getaways have you gone to?" Dee asked, knowing she had been on even more than Raquel (though only by one) because this was one of her most regular questions.

Still, everyone followed the script, starting with Kelso.

"I've done all of them inside eScape, unless they've added one I don't know about, and let's be real, how could that possibly happen? I did the Ruthless Sunshine Day Camp in real life, and as a family we did the Ibiza Getaway, plus Barbados when my parents had that tax thing."

Raquel went next. "A few in here, but those aren't as much fun. There's zero chance I'm going to meet him, and who wants to compete with all those other trollops in the comment sections? I've gone to Sydney, Carmel, New York, Austin, London, and Malibu four — no, *five* times because that one at least we can drive to."

It was always "four — no, *five* times."

Then Kam took her turn. "I've done everything in eScape, plus all the Ruthlessly Positive Childhood through Adolescence classes. And we did Hawaii every year."

Kam had done everything in eScape, but only because she was looking for clues. And she always said Hawaii; none of them had ever made her lies easier to bury. She answered on autopilot, barely there. Her friends were already back to comparing experiences, having moved beyond the part of the conversation where they flexed about where they'd gone, now onto how much each event had changed their lives. Kelso made the strongest argument, no doubt driven by his deficit in live transformations when compared to everyone else's.

Kam kept replaying her first conversation with Lyle on repeat, remembering the way he had eased his way over to their table and confronted her friends. That's what it had felt like, more so after replaying the frames and knowing who he really was. He argued anonymously, but Kam understood now what she didn't then. That Lyle couldn't keep quiet with that group spouting off so close to him. He needed to ridicule some of the same words that were leaving his mouth right now.

The man on the broadcast was all an act.

But it wasn't like Kam could say anything. Nobody knew the real Lyle, not like she did. Certainly none of the people in this room, and maybe not anywhere else in the whole world. There was his mother, of course, but Julia used her knowledge to control him.

Kam used to keep her mouth shut because she didn't want her rich eScape friends to know how different she really was. Not just from them, but from everyone. A quickly decaying body in real life, and a hacker with unlimited funds in here. But now … Kam was struggling to keep it all inside.

She wanted to open her mouth and let everything come pouring out. She longed to shout the truth: that Lyle didn't believe any of the bullshit he was spouting, not on this broadcast or any of the others, in here or out there in the real world. Ruthless Positivity had seeds of truth, and he kept them planted inside him to fertilize the rest. But like fertilizer, it was all just shit in the end.

Kam was sure that in reality, Lyle was only spewing nonsense because—

The wall went dark and an icy terror slithered inside her.

"What happened?" Dee and Raquel wondered out loud together.

"He's gone," Kelso said, stating the obvious.

He was right. The room behind Lyle was empty. The small boxes below his window showed a collection of crowds that were just as confused as Kam and her friends.

Everyone had to be wondering the same thing:

Who unplugged Lyle Grace?

Chapter Five

Lyle

—AN APPROXIMATE RESPONSE TIME *of nine minutes from now.*

Someone had unplugged Lyle from eScape.

It was so sudden and unexpected, he would be pissed if the world wasn't so blurry. Vox was chirping in his ears. It might have been yelling, but Lyle was still emerging from his Nest and the sound in his audio pickup was low, giving him time to let the dizziness and disorientation fade.

It was dangerous to yank someone out of a Deep Spell without their consent.

Lyle was out of the Nest and stumbling through the room, hands out to feel his way. He kept blinking, trying to recover both balance and sight while cursing his idiocy.

He should never have held the impromptu broadcast. It was stupid and impulsive. Exactly the type of thing Mother was always harping on him about. It's like he was trying to prove her right.

But it wasn't that at all. Lyle hadn't been able to stop thinking about Kam. Getting out on a live feed like that, he felt sure she would send him some sort of a signal. He spent the entire broadcast having Vox scroll through all the audience feeds to see if he could find her. But he never did, and now he was sucking air through his teeth while trying to slowly reorient himself with reality.

His vision finally cleared, but then his heart stopped.

Lyle couldn't believe his eyes. He blinked, but the mirage refused to go away. It had been two decades since the last time he'd seen this man, swaying and smiling at his son from behind a piss-drunk smile.

How did he get into his home? Had he broken a window? Followed an unsuspecting Lyle inside? Did he know Mother was off on one of her women-only retreats? And most horrifying of all, had he been watching him in the Nest all this time? That was disgusting if so, like standing in the shadows and watching someone take a shit.

Lyle's father abandoned them more than eighteen years ago, and had never even once tried to make contact with him since. What the hell was he doing here now?

That's what I've been trying to tell you. Vox in his ear, only now audible in a way that made any sense. *Your father is here.*

"What are you doing here?" Lyle asked.

He laughed. "Is that how you want to say hello to me after all these years?"

"I'm not obligated to say anything at all."

Vox chirped again. *I've already notified the police. They've given an approximate response time of seven minutes from now. Two since the initial estimate.*

Father took three long strides over to an older armchair that Lyle had bought secondhand because he kinda sorta liked it and it really pissed Mother off. He plopped down deep into the seat and turned to his son. Slurring his words, he said, "It has been a spell."

"You've been gone for twenty years."

"Eighteen." There was something indecipherable in his smile. Cold and menacing, but maybe heartbreaking as well. Lyle could only stare, and wonder how long it might take for the moment to pass. He sure as hell wouldn't be the one to break their silence.

He didn't last long. "Got anything to drink?"

"I don't drink," Lyle lied.

"Sure you do."

"Why are you here?"

"To reconnect. It's been too long."

"Why are you really here?"

He laughed. "To get what's coming to me."

The words were a blade in Lyle's shoulder, cutting him deep. He used to lie awake at night imagining a moment like this, when he'd finally get the chance to see his father again. He used to dream about the way it might happen, but never once had this scenario been part of his vision.

Not even after Lyle had learned to hate him. "And what is it you *think* you have coming to you?" He stared into his father's eyes without flinching.

"I've never been a greedy man, and I'm not about to start now that I'm dying." He shrugged. "A million credits oughta cover it."

You're dying?

But Lyle couldn't say that, or afford to care. "I don't have that kind of money. Even if I did, I'd never just hand it over to the person who abandoned me when I was only two years old, leaving us so you could live like a scumbag."

"That's what she told you, huh?" His father nodded appreciatively. "Makes sense."

"You need to get out of my house. The cops are on their way."

Another shrug. "I bet we have a few minutes still.

Wouldn't you like to catch up?" Then he chased a burp with a reeking, drunken laugh.

"I'm not giving you any money."

"I thought you didn't have any money."

"Not the kind you're asking for," Lyle said, working hard not to snarl. "But it doesn't make any difference, you're not getting a credit."

"Okay."

"Okay?"

"Okay," he repeated. "Then I guess I'll have no choice, I'll have to sue your mother."

Lyle laughed. "Sue her for what?"

He matched his son's laugh with a trio of bilious bursts. "Any one of the things I'm sure you don't know about."

"Why should I believe a word you say?"

"Because I'm sure you know your mother better than anyone by now. Even more than me. And if that's true, then I bet there's not many things I could say that would really surprise you."

Lyle swallowed. He didn't want to hear this. It was tempting to believe that his father was full of shit, but even piss drunk his unflinching eyes were gleaming with truth.

Four minutes, Vox said.

"The police will be here in a minute. You should go if you want to stay out of jail."

"Oh, I'm sure we have more than a minute. And I have ID to prove who I am. You think the cops are really going to arrest your father?"

"If you were breaking and entering, *yes*."

"Door was open. I walked right in."

He's lying.

"The AI record will say otherwise."

"Come on, Lyle. We're wasting time."

"Then tell me what you want."

"I told you: *one million credits.*"

"And I told you: *that's impossible.*"

"I thought that 'impossible is the hobgoblin of possibility.' Isn't that what you and your mother are always saying? What" — another laugh — "am I not being ruthless enough? You tell me what to do, then, Lyle, to get what I deserve."

"You think you *deserve* a million credits you didn't work for, just because you helped to spawn me? Why on—"

"No, *son.* I deserve a million credits because your mother is a human stain who poisoned me."

"What are you talking about?"

"She slipped Estravir into my food."

"What's that?"

He studied Lyle's face before answering. "A drug that makes the user more suggestible. Though, and you might find this hilarious, the user of this particular drug rarely if ever even knows they're partaking. I didn't, until I finally got my system flushed."

"Why would she do that?"

"She needed some way to wield her influence over me after I got a lot harder to control post-marriage. You know your mother."

Now Lyle was studying his father's face, searching and seeing no visible runes of dishonesty. "Why haven't I ever heard of this drug?"

"Estravir was illegal then and still is now. More so if that's possible. But I thought your mom might've figured out a way to buy some anyway, seeing as it's such a great way to get what she wants."

"What did she want from you?" Lyle asked.

And with the bitterest smile so far, he said, "For me to leave you alone with her forever."

Even if he had some idea of what to say, Lyle probably couldn't make the words.

His father continued. "Seemed like a good idea at the time. But then again, so did jumping off a bridge or swallowing the wrong end of a shotgun. I had a lot of awful ideas that didn't seem so awful, especially after your mother kept cranking up my dosage."

Lyle swallowed again, sensing the horror of what was to come.

"A lot of bad shit happened to me after that, son. It had to be done, but flushing all that Estravir out of my system led to a lot of other problems."

He stopped, forcing Lyle to ask. "Like what?"

"Like a loss of impulse control, reduced executive function, mental health issues. Long story short, I've spent a lot of my life in the loony bin. They gave me a drug to deal with the symptoms, and that worked well enough for a while. I stayed away from both of you, and kept the poison out of my life."

"So why are you here?" Lyle asked, with hate he maybe shouldn't feel.

"Because the drugs to fix what your mother ruined have led to a degenerative condition in my brain. I'm going to die without help, and treatment's expensive. So I'll be needing you to cover it."

"No treatment costs a million credits."

"You are right about that, son. But after the little story I just shared with you, I'm sure we can agree that a little interest is fair."

Lyle shook his head. "I already told you, I don't have that kind of money."

"Even if you don't, you're a lot closer to it than me. Unless you prefer the lawsuit route. This case will pay out a lot more than a million credits in court. But you don't want to go that way and neither do I. Given all the time in the world, sure, I'd love to ruin your mother. But I need the money faster than that, and I know how long she'll keep me tied up in court."

Even if he was lying, a lawsuit would ruin everything. Not just the financial impact of a trial, they would be able to weather that, including a payout. It was the hit to their reputation that would really ruin Ruthlessly Positive and its bottom line if his father's truth was ever made public.

"Vox: Cancel the police."

Are you—

"Yes, Vox. I'm sure."

"Smart move," his father said with a nod.

"I'm not doing it for you."

"Understood." Another nod.

"Why aren't you dealing with her directly?"

"We both know she can't be trusted."

"I need a couple of days," Lyle said.

"Of course you do." His father stood and started walking toward the door. "I can see myself out."

"How am I supposed to get in touch with you?"

"You wait." He closed the door behind him, leaving Lyle alone with himself.

Or at least mostly alone. "Vox, which accounts do I have access to, even if Mother notices that funds are missing?"

Might I suggest an alternative course of action?

"You might."

What about a reconciliation?

"I don't know what you mean by that."

You can use the power of Ruthless Positivity to publicly heal your relationship.

Lyle was about to protest, because he wanted to keep this as far away from Mother as possible, but then he got it.

"This could be the start of my own career, separate from Mother. If my message is all about father-son relationships, then she can't have any part of that. I could branch out from Ruthless Positivity and finally start talking about things that matter to me."

Julia will hate it.

"She sure will." A cocktail of dread and excitement slowly settled inside him.

He fell deeper into thought. Practically shuddering at the edge of a life change he was eagerly horrified to make.

Lyle?

"Yep?"

I hesitate to bring this up, but …

"You don't hesitate to bring anything up, Vox. Stop with the drama, not just now but forever, and tell me whatever it is you want to tell me."

The girl, from yesterday.

"What about her?"

You did seem to like her.

"She was fine."

You had me scan the feeds looking for her.

Lyle didn't answer.

She was nice, and did seem to appreciate you for you.

Still Lyle said nothing.

You did seem to like her, Vox repeated. *Or am I wrong about that?*

"I said she was fine."

But Lyle had liked her. A lot. Until she started bragging about how rich she was, revealing that regardless of her initial front, she was the same as all the other materialistic people who populated his life, and Mother's seminars. He would be an idiot to reconnect with her, no matter how much he wanted to.

I have a suggestion.

"Great," Lyle said, as though he didn't want to know.

Invite her to your live event.

"Why would I do that?"

Because you need closure. She'll either do something to kill whatever attraction remains, or prove herself worthy of your attention. You win, no matter what.

Lyle wasn't sure about that logic, but he agreed anyway.

Why not? He would be organizing this event by himself. A first, since this time he wouldn't be following one of the usual scripts. It wasn't like Lyle's audience would believe Kam, even if she did try to out his secret identity inside eScape.

"Get her an invite, with a pass to the VIP event afterward."

Of course, Vox said.

Even though he knew it would hurt him later, Lyle started to dream.

And tried not to think about all the ways it could go wrong.

Chapter Six

Kam

KAM HAD to keep smothering the butterflies.

They were out of control, fluttering in her stomach, relentless.

She couldn't remember the last time she felt so inexplicably nervous. There was no reason for the anxiety; it wasn't like Kam was crashing the event uninvited. According to Pibly, she was practically a VIP. Lyle hadn't reached out himself, but his AI assistant had. This felt like a second chance to make everything right, and maybe reset the board to where it was before she'd been awkward enough to mess it all up with her moronic and unrelenting mouth.

Kam kept looking around, afraid that she'd see Kelso, Raquel, and Dee, all in a huddle without her. Of course they would be attending, but she couldn't afford for them to see her there, especially as a special guest.

Lyle was holding a special event. A surprise, just like the last one, except also entirely different. He promised new content. Pibly pressed Vox for more information, and from one AI to another, Lyle's assistant promised that they were in for something epic. Kam kept wondering what that could mean, and what he might be sharing. It seemed to her that Julia closely monitored her son's communication with his audience, which she obviously saw as *theirs*. But unlike Lyle's last impromptu seminar, the tone of this event seemed outside of the usual Ruthlessly Positive fare.

Despite her nerves, Kam couldn't wait to see where this might be going. The police force inside eScape were always active and seldom out of sight. But today they were thicker than usual, and she made sure to give them a wide berth as she went about her way.

Technically, nothing was illegal within the digital space, which meant that all sorts of dangerous activities had no repercussions because everything could be virtually fixed. The police were there to watch out for people hacking into eScape's infrastructure, harming users in some way, or taking advantage of the system. They were tasked with preventing hacks within the space and maintaining the construct's integrity. Keeping it safe from users like Kam.

She approached Lyle's pavilion, her heart pounding harder than she wanted it to. Letting her know that she was very much alive. A pair of milkshakes, one in each hand. Chocolate and vanilla, so Lyle could choose. She hoped he would think it was cute, and maybe even romantic. But the part of Kam that always had her doubt working overtime was sure he'd think she was stupid.

She tightened her grip on the milkshakes and walked faster, ignoring the shrewish voice in her head. There wasn't any reason for her to feel such a deeply seated uncertainty. Lyle had invited her, she had a ticket to attend this event — a special request by the presenter himself.

So what if she had never been good at this kind of

thing? She didn't need to be. Kam was doing her job just by showing up. Lyle wouldn't think the shakes were stupid, he would see them as the peace offering they were.

She paused outside the pavilion.

Maybe you shouldn't go inside just yet, Pibly suggested.

"Why?"

Your anxiety levels are high.

"I know my anxiety levels are high," Kam said in her lowest possible voice.

Visibly noticeable. I mean I don't think you'll want Lyle to see you this way.

Pibly could be such a know-it-all, but it was also right more often than not.

"Fine." She looked down at her milkshakes, wanting to steal a sip from each of them.

Circle the pavilion. The trip around might be enough to calm you down.

Kam didn't want to do that, but wasn't brazen enough to ignore Pibly without cause. She just wished she didn't look like such a git, walking around with a milkshake in each hand. At least they wouldn't melt inside eScape.

She was halfway around the pavilion when she spied her friends in the VIP area around back.

Kam ducked behind a wide pillar, then peeked back to make sure that she hadn't been spotted. They had invited her along. Dee said it wouldn't be the same with just the three of them. Raquel practically begged her, saying she'd needed Kam because she would be a "great wingman, or woman as it were." Raquel was the most delusional of Kam's three eScape friends, truly believing that she and Lyle were destined for one another, if only fate could get them in a room together.

Kam stuck to her guns, rejecting her friends' invitation with regret, telling them that she would, and that she really wanted to, but she had already made plans with Chad and wouldn't feel right cancelling them at the last minute. They understood and supported her reasoning. All three of them loved hearing her dish about their adventurous dates, especially Kelso and Raquel, even though there wasn't really a Chad and Kam always had to manufacture every moment of their escapades.

No one was surprised when Kam said she couldn't attend Lyle's seminar. That was her usual pattern. She always had plans with Chad when there was something she didn't want to do with the group, but that was especially true if their desired activities had anything to do with Ruthlessly Positive. Her friends were all obsessed, but Kam could only take those experiences in the smallest of doses. Too much PTSD, her childhood trauma falling like hail on her head. It would have been easier to find friends who didn't care about Julia Grace, her son, or their "life-changing" program. But in reality that was one of the biggest draws of her relationship with Kelso, Raquel, and Dee in the first place. She was allergic to fire, and a pyromaniac anyway.

Kam knew the base-level curriculum inside out, so she could hold her own in every conversation, but her friends also liked to tease her about talking the talk without walking the walk. She was happy to let them. They understood her allegiance to Chad, he had one hell of an imaginary profile, after all. From his stats to the design of his body and face. But Kam knew they also got a sense of smug superiority from being more devoted fans of Ruthless Positivity than she was. That perception preserved her secret identity, so Kam was happy to let her friends think whatever they wanted to.

But still, the last thing she wanted was to get spotted right now. Without Chad, and a pair of milkshakes. Her friends were glancing around, taking it all in, leaving her feeling exposed, and making it difficult to get back to the pavilion entrance.

"I need a route out of here," she mumbled to Pibly.

Might I suggest—

"Never mind, I know where to go."

Kam left the pillar and took several long strides until she was surrounded by a group of raving fans, or *fanatics* was more like it. They were all wide-eyed. Most were screaming, several at the top of their lungs. Kam imagined the Ruthless Positivity Kool-Aid dripping from their chins. It was mind-numbing being buried in their circle, but at least for now she was safe from exposure.

Perhaps you should try harder to fit in.

Pibly's words hit her ears and Kam realized how ridiculous she must look. Standing amid all those screaming fans with her dour expression, clutching a couple of milkshakes and probably looking like she'd rather be anywhere else in the world.

Fans of the program were understandably ruthless. If this group saw her looking like a tourist, they'd gladly rip her apart.

So she followed Pibly's suggestion and screamed with delight. Whooping and hollering, yelling at the top of her lungs to let the world know how much she loved Ruthlessly Positive.

Danger. Your anger levels are—

She didn't need the warning. Kam's rage was immediate, claiming her at a cellular level. A flash of exasperation burning into pure and undiluted fury, thick enough to smother her.

Kam kept screaming, but the tenor had changed, fueled by the memory of those times her father had dragged her to seminars, when she was given no choice but to paste a vacuous smile on her innocent face, forced to feign her belief in the bullshit.

Kam had been raised to shove her feelings into a box, then close the lid and keep it locked. Once inside they could never, ever eScape.

Throttling those emotions was a lot harder than it used to be. She needed to get out of there without being spotted, but her friends were even closer than before and Kam had no means of eScape. She couldn't stop her thoughts:

This is stupid and I hate it and I can't stand my friends for buying into any of this!

But at least she knew how to fight back.

The truth is pure and rarely simple.

Then another three times to lock the message into her brain.

The truth is pure and rarely simple.
The truth is pure and rarely simple.
The truth is pure and rarely simple.

The velvet rope was lifted and her friends were finally ushered away from the rest of the plebes and into the VIP section, where a single seat cost more credits than Kam received after a full year of government-mandated disability.

She ignored the truth of it making her sick, squeezed her numb fingers around the still-frozen milkshake, and followed Pibly's directions as he deftly guided her back to the pavilion entrance.

She should have ignored her anxiety and gone in the first time. Now there was a riot of people and activity. Service workers in an endless line, hauling props and equipment in and out of the tent for the great Lyle Grace and his crew.

What had she been thinking, bringing these milkshakes? That was about her, not about him.

What did she expect, that he would stop everything he was doing before his big event, so he could sit down and share a milkshake with her?

Or guzzle his own since Kam had apparently brought a pair of them?

She was a stupid idiot and deserved any ridicule that might be coming her way.

The truth is pure and rarely simple.
The truth is pure and rarely simple.
The truth is pure and rarely simple.

She was lucky to have gotten an invitation. Lyle was being nice to her, maybe even trying to butter her up into keeping his secret.

But there wasn't any more to it than that, and Kam had been a fool to think so.

She looked around for a place to toss her milkshakes, feeling more and more pissed at herself.

She spied a bank of trash cans in the distance, but there were throngs of people standing between it and her. They might not even be real; some of them might be bots to make the place look fuller than it actually was.

But then Kam realized what it was she was actually seeing, and asked Pibly to please confirm.

That is correct. The assembled party is populated by a group of vendors seeking endorsement possibilities for the event.

Perfect. Owning the Malt Shoppe made her a vendor, and Kam was used to pretending anyway.

If only every part of her wasn't sure that she was about to mess everything up.

Chapter Seven

Lyle

MAYBE THIS WASN'T such a good idea.

Lyle kept thinking the same thing on repeat while watching his father smiling his way through a long line of diehard fans and glad-handers. He was a different man sober, though what did Lyle know? Besides pictures and videos. The memories were barely there, and the few he had felt like a lie.

Looking at him now, chatting at the edge of the stage with some members of the press, Lyle's reps, and sponsors, it was easy to picture his parents together. Lyle could imagine his parents working the crowd in unison. Maybe that's the way it should have been; maybe then she would have been able to leave Lyle alone long enough to give him a decent childhood.

Instead he'd been forced to play husband number two. The truth, once he started to understand it, had always made him shudder.

He needed to pull his father in, but Lyle only made it a

single step in his direction before he was floored by the sight of Kam. He was surprised by how happy he felt to see her, though maybe it was the way she was showing up. Overwhelmed more than anything else, like a lost little girl. Her hands were each filled with a milkshake from the Malt Shoppe, Lyle was touched that she'd spent the energy to haul them all the way here. The more items you carried, the quicker your vitality was depleted.

He turned away from his father and approached Kam instead.

She brightened at the sight, and her arm lurched forward with what looked like an involuntary thrust, holding one of the shakes out in offering. "It's chocolate … unless you want vanilla." She switched arms, the other floundering toward him. "I wanted you to have a choice …"

She looked around, still overwhelmed, what seemed to be a deluge of emotions multiplying her freckles, and widening her eyes in wonder and innocence.

"But I guess that was dumb," she finally finished. "You have so much going on here."

Lyle only invited her because of Vox, but things tended to go well when he followed his AI's advice. Still, standing in front of her now, looking ever so slightly down into a gaze that felt fixed on his, life itself seemed somehow louder inside him.

She'd barely spoken, but his body felt warmer already.

"It's not dumb at all." He took the chocolate.

"I just wanted to apologize … for the other day."

Lyle wasn't sure what she was sorry for, but he enjoyed the tune of her brewing apology.

When he didn't respond she explained.

"I was just so surprised once I realized who you were, I

got really insecure … I started babbling … I do that and … well, I'm sorry that I—"

"It's fine." He smiled and raised a hand to stop her. "It happens all the time."

"I can imagine."

Lyle could practically smell her sincerity, and appreciated her apology, but he didn't want her to be sorry at all, and if she was going to be rueful about anything, it should be for all that empty boasting.

It was another stabbing truth, that he could never find someone who liked Lyle for Lyle, instead of Lyle Grace the junior-celebrity. Not because of anything he'd done or earned for himself. He was the offspring of genius, according to the press.

Kam was a nice normal girl, like the kind Lyle had always wanted. Until she discovered who he was. She got weird after finding out, and it was still a little weird now.

He couldn't change the way she looked at him, but Lyle could finally start claiming for himself. Things would be different after this event, and he was starting to feel the evolution already.

After several seconds of lingering silence, Kam said, "This must be costing you a fortune."

"I'm sorry?"

She looked around, gesturing at the massive crowd, and all the people scurrying about. "Putting on an event like this. I can't imagine the tab on this thing."

Another smile, this one to honor the way she surprised him. "For sure. But no one's ever said anything like that to me before."

"Like what?" Kam asked.

"Everyone always talks about how rich we must be, Mother and me. People rarely ever realize or even think about how much gets reinvested back into the business of helping people."

Lyle could hear the lie as he said it. Not for him, he really was going out on a limb, using six months of his stash to pull this all off, even after the sponsorships. It wasn't a paid event, and unlike eScape broadcasts scheduled and sanctioned by Mother, this was off the books and therefore coming out of his pocket. A pop-up event he announced on the fly at a time when he could be reasonably certain Mother wouldn't be paying attention.

But he could be wrong, or someone might tell her sooner rather than later. Either way, Lyle would have to deal with her once this was over.

Telling Kam that *people rarely ever realize or even think about how much has to get reinvested back into the business of helping people* was Lyle repeating his mother's lies through his new and necessary filter of truth. That was the story Mother had told him to explain why their money went into accounts that only she had access to. The question had lived in the recesses of his mind for a while, but Kam's query got it floating back on the surface.

"I understand," she said.

"I guess you would," Lyle agreed. Maybe he was being unfair. "I guess anybody with money has had to deal with their fair share of gold diggers."

"Yeah." Her lone word sounded like a cough.

He meant it as a compliment. But the change on her face and in her posture suggested that wasn't how she took it. She shifted on her feet and looked anxiously around.

"Is there something I can help you find?" Lyle asked.

"No." An awkward smile. "Thanks … I'm sorry, it's just—"

"I understand," Lyle said, realizing in the moment that he most certainly did.

Of course he had made her uncomfortable talking about gold diggers. Some man in her past had tried to exploit her for money, after she'd finally made it on her own, after her father's death. It was probably awful for her, and Lyle was sorry that had happened, but in a way he felt grateful. Knowing what he now knew made him feel much more comfortable around her. They were more alike than he'd realized.

Lyle could see it in her eyes: *Does he really understand?*

They held their stare until she finally sighed with what felt like the exhale he'd been waiting for.

"It looks like you're needed," Kam said, gesturing to the crowd of waiting press, his father standing before them, the entire crowd turned expectantly toward Lyle. "Who is that man?"

"Baker Grace. My father."

"YOUR FATHER?"

"Shhh … yes, keep it down, please. That's supposed to be a big announcement."

"How long have the two of you been talking?"

"A few days."

"You haven't seen him since you were what … two years old?"

"That's right." He nodded. This was a well-documented part of the story that had made Mother more than a hundred million credits, many of which belonged to Lyle despite his not having them.

"Is that what this event is all about, you patching things up with your dad?"

Lyle nodded again.

He couldn't say much because Kam wouldn't understand. Yes, there was reconciliation, but it was also smart marketing. So long as Father played the part, there was a genuine opportunity here. Father seemed to be behaving himself. And sober, he had a rugged charm. Perfect for the role of repentant absentee dad who had seen the error of his ways and now wanted to make things right with the child he abandoned all those years ago. The press would gobble it up like strawberry cobbler in season. There were few storylines better than a reunion drama, and while Ruthlessly Positive had been mining its audience for years to unearth such narratives, Lyle now had one of his own.

Mother would be furious, even if it boosted her sales, which of course it would. But pissing her off was probably his biggest bonus of all.

There was only so much Lyle could do. It wasn't like Mother could be angry with him in public. What would it look like to the world if she seemed upset by a reunion between her son and his father? The slightest ire might destroy her career.

Mother would have no choice but to finally hear him out. She couldn't keep all his money, like prisoners of the silent civil war he'd been fighting for most of his life. The battles were finally about to be over. Soon, he wouldn't even have to live in the same country as her. Once Lyle had his trust, he could use the funds to live and build his own business. This was a big win for him, assuming he could see it through and stand up for what was so obviously right.

"How does it feel? You know, meeting your father after all this time?"

"Weird for sure, but also great." Lyle smiled.

He couldn't say more without losing his shit.

Meaning, the guilt would come. Because no, Lyle wasn't really being honest. The last three days with Baker Grace had been illuminating for sure. Lyle had gotten to know his father better than he expected to, but he didn't exactly like what he'd seen.

Lyle kept reminding himself to focus on what was most important. He would cover his father's treatment, then kick the man back out of his life.

They didn't need to be best friends. Their reconciliation was real in the ways that would benefit his audience. Lyle did want to help people with their relationships, so the whitest of lies was fine. Yes, he was using Mother's logic, and yes, that made Lyle sick to his stomach. But there was a big difference between her and him. A lone fib was fine, if he promised to tell the truth about everything else.

He glanced back at Baker and the press, gave them an affirmative nod — *just another second, be right there* — then turned back to Kam.

"You've gotta go," she said.

"I do." Lyle nodded. "But first I wanted to take you up on your offer, if it's still available."

"My offer?"

"The Palisades."

"Oh." She smiled. "Of course. Do you really want to go?"

"I've been thinking about you, and I'd really love to talk. You know ... away from all of this."

"That sounds ..." Kam paused and time seemed to slow as she considered the rest of her answer. Lyle hoped it took a while, because once she finished their moment would be broken and he'd be onto the difficult work of designing an unforgettable experience for everyone here.

"That sounds perfect," she finally finished.

Her delight stole his breath. Lyle finally recovered by clearing his throat, offering Kam another smile, then tipping his head and walking away toward Baker and the press.

He turned back and called back to her over his shoulder. "I'll see you at the private after-party!"

He would remember her smile until then.

And he did, keeping Kam front-of-mind while fielding questions next to Baker, though most of Lyle's responses were simple enough: *Wait for broadcast.*

He also kept it in mind as his usual crew hurried him backstage to prepare for the main event. They would be protected from Mother's wrath in the aftermath because they would have no way of knowing the event was unsanctioned. Lyle Grace himself gave the go-ahead, after all. Pop-ups like this, as opposed to the more structured workshops and summits, worked with the younger people in eScape, and Lyle was usually the one to run these things in here.

Still, his mother would want to know why he'd done this.

And he kept it in mind as he took the stage, searching for Kam in the fifth row, over on the right side where Vox had inconspicuously sat her. Not too far, and not too close, knowing Mother would be inspecting the footage later, searching for clues that might explain her son's betrayal.

Ten seconds, Vox warned him.

Lyle had never felt so centered.

Seven … six …

It was time to reunite with his father and take his career to a whole new level.

Five … four …

One where he'd never need Mother for money or basic survival ever again.

Three … two …

Everything was about to change.

And one. Good luck.

The red curtain rose, and minutes later Lyle knew exactly how much he needed it.

Chapter Eight

Kam

KAM LOOKED over to the VIP section where her friends were all giggling like school girls, including the lone boy in their threesome. She sank lower in her chair, grateful that Lyle had seated her in such an inconspicuous spot, with seven rows laid out like a shield before her.

She was in the perfect place to observe without being noticed. She felt like a bird on its perch, able to watch Dee and Raquel each playing with their side of Kelso's shaggy, nearly shoulder-length hair. Kam couldn't afford to be seen. The lying always made her sick, and when it came to Ruthless Positivity, she found herself uncharacteristically negative. She stopped talking. Even her listening turned resentful, searching for the other side of every word.

If they discovered her now, sitting all by herself after refusing to join them under the charade of yet another unmissable outing with Chad, Kam wasn't sure what would be leaving her mouth.

Surely the bullshit would be worthy of Julia Grace.

Her heart started pounding the second the lights began to dim and energetic music swelled. She shouldn't be this invested, but there wasn't a thing in the world Kam could do to stop herself. Not right now.

She leaned forward with a tingling body, needing to see what was now only seconds away.

The red curtain rose, looking practically black in the dark. A border of soft lights barely illuminated Lyle as he stepped out onto the stage, then brightened as he made his way to the edge, music swelling in time with his appearance.

Kam was glad for the riotous crowd, quieting the beating of her heart against her ribcage.

Why was she so attracted to him?

Why was the very sight of Lyle enough to make her cross her legs and then cross them again?

Why was she curling her toes, dreaming about seeing him out after the show at a private party and maybe in a secluded room, and generally acting like the little lovesick girl that she wasn't?

Most of all, why was she so terrified of screwing up again?

Probably because Kam had always known that she and Lyle were meant for each other. She just didn't think that would ever actually happen. Not with so many social walls standing between them, in both the real world and virtual worlds.

But Kam found a place where she could knock all of hers down, then destiny sent her true love into the Malt Shoppe, a business owned by her, honest or not.

Now she felt crippled by the prospect of ruining it.

She settled in the seat and watched Lyle patiently wait for his applause to die.

His smile turned into something more serious, immediately getting to business. "You've heard me talk a lot about manifesting love by eliminating your negativity and …" He waited a beat for another round of mild applause. "And I'm very proud to share with you an example of how that's recently happened in my own life. An example I'm hoping you can use to change your life, too. And I mean that for every one of you watching."

But Kam could swear she felt his eyes settling on her. Boring into her, like a drill bit turning the earth. He held their shared gaze just long enough, then went on when she wished he wouldn't.

The moment for her had gone missing, and in its place she heard the empty platitudes that had colored the nothingness she felt in each module from every course she'd ever been forced to take from the ridiculously named and even more absurdly executed Ruthlessly Positive.

Lyle reminded everyone watching that his version of enlightenment came as part of a five-step process. He reminded them all that negativity was the offspring of fear, and that an awareness led to the elimination of a person's worst possible thoughts. And finally, Lyle reminded his audience that the Cosmos of Totality were a genie in the bottle, but only once you knew how and where to rub your best intentions.

Lyle looked out at the crowd. Again his eyes settled on hers, but this time she didn't want them to. "That upset feeling you have in your stomach … where do you think that's coming from?"

Same place as always, she thought.

Kam couldn't help her irritation. This was the same shit as always. Julia wasn't here, so what was he doing? He didn't need to lie. It was getting harder and harder to hear, and watch. She listened for some actual meaning but there was nothing there, and it felt like walls were closing in on either side of her. The Lyle who doubted that his mother's work was for everyone versus the Lyle who preached a hundred percent positivity.

A ball of fire burned inside her.

Kam turned from Lyle's stare, no longer able to stand it.

When she looked back several seconds later, he had already turned away and was walking to the other side of the stage. They weren't even ten minutes in, and already too many emotions were warring within her. She hated the déjà vu, but it gripped her insides, squeezing hard, a scream clawing its way up her throat. It felt like barbed wire as she swallowed it.

Kam bit her lip and curled her toes. Imagined dragging the tip of a knife down her leg. She needed the distraction. And besides, the temporary pain of bleeding was little compared to the ever-present agony of shame that had followed Kam like a shadow for almost every day of her life.

Shame for not believing.

Shame for not being able to root out the weeds of negativity in her soul that wouldn't stop growing.

Shame for how much she hated her father for always putting her on display and forcing her to say the words.

Memories rained and Kam hated them for making her hate so much of herself.

It wasn't her fault, none of it was. It was *his*, for always punishing her, no matter how hard she tried. For making her feel like there wasn't much of a difference between her best and worst efforts.

For always calling her a bad seed.

Endless hours Kam had spent on her knees in the reflection room, and hers wasn't exactly well-appointed. Kelso's reflection room was divvied into six separate spaces, one for each member of his family. It was bigger than her entire house, not that any of them knew that. Months of hours spent chafing her knees, reciting positive affirmations that were supposed to cleanse her soul yet only made her long to vomit instead.

"I've kept you waiting long enough," Lyle announced to the crowd.

Kam agreed, still sitting anxiously in her seat.

"You know so much of my story. Now are you ready to see how I've manifested love in my life?"

The crowd roared with a deafening *YES!*

Lyle turned stage left and beckoned into the darkness.

The man Kam had already seen from a distance took a tentative step onto the stage, scanned the crowd, then made several long strides until he was finally standing by Lyle's side.

"I'd like you all to meet Baker Grace, my father."

The crowd issued a collective gasp. A pregnant second, then thunderous applause as the music returned.

Lyle waited for the music to fade again. "I'm sure some of you can imagine how hard I must have worked to stay Ruthlessly Positive in the face of abandonment. No matter how many times I told myself it wasn't true, my deepest self was sure that I wasn't good enough for my own father to love me."

Lyle paused, as soft piano played, milking every emotion. He took a long moment to look at the man who had abandoned him, but his expression wasn't filled with accusation or anger. The only emotion on his face was love, and that felt like a strike of lightning in her soul.

Kam clenched her fists and imagined a blade dragging its way down her leg again. Under her breath she muttered, "I hate Julia Grace and I want her to die."

Then, *The truth is pure and rarely simple*, over and over and over.

"This week has been a new era for me and my father. And now it's a new era for all of us."

Kam wondered what that meant. Suspected that she knew.

"I might be the most Ruthlessly Positive man in the world—"

Another thought that made her want to vomit.

"—after being raised with the belief system for as long as I can remember. Mother has always taken such excellent care of me, making sure I become the man I was always supposed to be. Thanks to the reunion with my father, now I finally know what that means."

Kam wondered if he was only a puppet standing on the stage like a big boy without any strings, or if they would get to hear from Baker Grace himself.

"But as of today, I'll be taking everything I've learned from a lifetime of working with Mother, and branching off to start something of my own. I will continue the important work we've been doing together, but with an element that is unique to me. The male population can do better in this world, and that all starts with better father-son relationships. Regardless of your gender, this work will help you. If you have a brother or a boyfriend who can do better, spread the word. Love truly does conquer all. Instead of being angry with my dad for leaving, I am choosing to love him."

The men embraced as the crowd erupted in its most thunderous round of applause so far, and Kam continued to throttle her fury.

She was growing angrier by the second, and was now considering standing up from her seat and marching out of there. She couldn't really do that, but right now Kam hated Lyle as much as she hated herself.

For not being able to be Ruthlessly Positive when it came to her own father, who she actively hated until her illness started, and by then she'd been so robbed of energy the only emotion she could muster was a form of defeated resignation.

For not avoiding yet another seminar filled with screaming sycophants and flunkies.

But most of all, Kam hated herself for not expecting something like this to happen. For believing he might be different.

Lyle seemed to be staring right through her. What made Kam want to swoon before now made her want to scream. He had been sympathetic the other day in private. But right now it felt like Lyle was publicly shaming Kam for not being able to love her abusive father with all of her heart.

Suffocating with rage, Kam could no longer stay in her seat.

She stood and scrambled through her row and into the aisle, turned away from Lyle so she couldn't see if he spied her flight from the pavilion.

She stumbled outside and over to a trash can. Lost her vomit inside it, then kept on hurling until her heaves turned dry and she hobbled way from the receptacle with an empty yet still acidic stomach.

Kam sat on the nearest bench and worked to recover her regular breath.

In and out, in and out, shoving the anger and panic down yet again.

But still, she couldn't shake it. She couldn't make herself numb like usual, no matter how hard she tried.

And the thought of going back inside the pavilion and facing Lyle made her want to revisit the garbage can.

She took out her phone to send him a message he wouldn't get until later.

Sorry, I got sick. Probably too much time in Deep Spell. I have to log out now, but I hope we can talk tomorrow.

She erased the period after *tomorrow*, traded it for an exclamation mark, then doubted herself and traded it back for the original period.

Kam pressed *Send* and cursed herself for ruining everything yet again.

Chapter Nine

Lyle

THE SHOW ENDED and Lyle hurried backstage.

He needed a shower, and not the sort of luxury romp with a waterfall in some artificial paradise like the kind he could pay for in eScape — Lyle wanted an old-fashioned scrub down where he could scrape the filth from every molecule of his body.

Lyle couldn't have felt any dirtier after doing what he'd just done for the last eighty-six minutes, answering one imbecilic question after another, stuck in an exhausting and at least semi-dishonest loop. Ugly but necessary to get him where he needed to go. And for once, it was okay, thanks to the North Star he had sitting eight rows back.

Until she disappeared not even halfway through his broadcast.

Lyle kept telling himself it was fine, that Kam knew what he was doing and wanted no part of it, she was of course waiting in the private room for him, eager for it all to end so they could finally look into one another's eyes and bask in their shared reality. They both knew the truth, and it would be like pulling a splinter out of his soul once he could finally say it out loud.

But he had to deal with his father first. It was exhausting, pretending there weren't two toxic decades between them, beaming whenever the press aimed their cameras his way, feeling his fraudulence like a sunburn on his back.

Kam would make it all go away.

She was the only one in the world who could understand him. It didn't make sense, how immediately bonded he felt. Perhaps that was just further proof of how little life he had outside of his mother — the first authentic person he'd connected with in forever consumed most of his thoughts. This couldn't be normal or healthy, but what did he know about either?

He needed to pass his father off to security, and get to the room where Lyle was sure she'd be waiting. He'd tell her the whole story, then she could assure him that everything would be okay.

"What do you mean you're leaving me?" Baker asked.

"You need to lower your voice." Lyle nodded at the clusters of press and attendees still milling about. "We already talked about this. Your work here is done. People have seen what I needed them to see."

"They'll want to see follow-up."

"I can tell stories. Starting with, 'My father is a very private man.'"

Baker smirked. "What about my money?"

"Nothing's changed. I can't give you anything until Mother transfers my trust."

"What if that doesn't happen?"

"It will."

"What if it doesn't?" Baker pressed.

Lyle shifted on his feet. This was asinine; he needed to

get the hell out of here, and over to the private area where Kam was surely waiting. "Then we'll deal with it then."

"I'm not going anywhere." Baker shook his head and crossed his arms. Still sober but now without his charm. Lyle saw only what he was: a petulant mess of a man. "You promised me a million credits."

"I told you to keep it down." Then in a whisper: "Even *one* person overhears us and the deal is off."

"Oh, I doubt you wanna do that," Baker said with a menacing smile.

"I have things to do, and you need to leave. I'll get you your money, soon as I can."

"You're right, that's fair. Let's start with a down payment. Say a hundred grand."

Lyle shook his head, growing increasingly agitated. "You're not getting it. Mother has my money locked up — *I don't have anything to give you until she finally turns it over to me.*"

"Bullshit." Father looked around at all the people. "I'm sure you made a fortune here today."

"This was a free event."

"Sure, for most of these suckers, but what about the idiots who paid for the VIP section — you telling me all the screaming girls behind the velvet rope were sitting there for free?"

"They paid, but this entire event was set up with our regular crew, using all of our usual systems, including for payment." Father just stood there looking at him, so Lyle went ahead and finished his thought. "That means Mother got the money, even though I held the event. It cost me to pull this thing off, and yet I'm not seeing a dime. I *lost* money on this. Lost money to help you. So again: *you'll get your money when I do.*"

Baker scoffed, looking Lyle up and down. "You don't

sound like someone who's reconciled with his estranged father. You sure you wanna be talking to me like this?"

"Is that a threat?"

He shrugged. "I don't know, Lyle, is it?"

They stood there staring at one another, a son refusing to dignify his disingenuous father, only back to get what he could after spending Lyle's childhood away, both holding their smiles as the crowd observed them like monkeys at the zoo.

Lyle finally answered in a whisper, soft and even slightly kind.

"I shouldn't have to remind you that if you do anything to ruin the perfect reunion story that we just sold the world on, *all the money goes away*. Our business will be ruined, especially my part of it. I made a promise and meant what I said, but if you don't give me the chance to make things happen, then I can amend my promise right now to one where I swear on everything I own that you won't get any—"

"Fine." Baker pulled him into an embrace and with a bellow he said, "I love you, son!" Then in a much softer voice that only Lyle could hear he added, "I think I'll go ahead and chat with some of the reporters. But don't worry" — he pulled away and winked — "I'll keep our little secret."

Then Baker turned around and walked away before his son could respond.

Lyle ignored everything he was feeling, confident that he could clear his conscious with Kam.

He rushed to the private room, weaving through the crowd without making eye contact with anyone, not willing to stop or be stopped on his way, needing to see and speak with Kam more than he could remember needing anything else for the longest time.

But she wasn't in the room, or anywhere around it.

When Lyle went back inside to check again and she still wasn't there, he had to force the panic out of his body. He took out his phone, and sure enough there was a message.

Sorry, I got sick. Probably too much time in Deep Spell. I have to log out now, but I hope we can talk tomorrow.

He read it three times, but the text never changed.

Kam wasn't here. She got sick. And he could feel the truth like bile in his stomach — she wasn't ill because she had spent too long in a Deep Spell; it had to be something he said.

I made her sick.

He collapsed into one of the room's giant chairs, looking over to the empty one next to him that should have been holding Kam.

Lyle closed his eyes, needing a drink, trying not to think about the obligations ahead. It was easier to deal with when he imagined Kam at his side, maybe holding his hand as he waded through the onslaught of fanatics who'd shelled out an insane number of credits just to spend some time with him at a private party.

The soiree would be starting soon, and he'd give anything to miss it. Lyle wished he was in his private Nest, instead of the one at Mother's Roost. He longed to be back in Jaxon, instead of this avatar the world already knew about. He wanted to meet up with Kam, at The Palisades or wherever else she wanted to go inside eScape. Or in real life.

Lyle heard the door open, followed by the clacking of heels on the hardwood.

He opened his eyes and turned toward the threshold with a smile, naive enough to believe he'd see Kam, hopeful that she was feeling better and was eager to see him.

But Lyle saw his nightmare instead of the dream.

Mother paused halfway between her son and the door, looking down at his lazy body sprawled in the chair. An emerald green dress made her look like a huntress, highlighting the dark sparkle in her predatory eyes. She smiled, perfect rows of bright white teeth gleaming, even brighter in this world than they would in the real one.

Yet, Lyle could see the heat of pure fury bubbling beneath her perfectly icy demeanor.

"We need to talk," she said.

"Of course we do." And goddammit, he still really needed that drink.

"Not here."

"Where do you want to talk?"

"Outside of eScape."

He shook his head. "I can't leave. I have an after-party starting in a few minutes."

"You're sick. We'll issue refunds. This isn't a request."

Lyle stared up at his mother, trying to determine which of his options sounded worse. Having it out, or faking his way through yet another VIP party. Even assuming he had a choice, which really he didn't if he wanted control of the trust, Lyle figured the verbal melee with Mother bested the event — it had to happen eventually and would change his life once it did.

"Fine. I'll see you—"

But Mother was already gone, out of eScape and back at home in her Roost.

He drew a deep breath, preparing himself for what was about to happen. It was never easy going in and out of eScape. The disorientation and the physical toll, the battle between outright exhaustion clanging against the energy of new experiences, all of it tinged his ambition. Each secret trip inside and away from Mother helped him to see the world in his own way, separate from the one she'd force-fed Lyle all his life. Despite its artifice, eScape felt more authentic to Lyle than life outside of it, and thus his departure often felt like mourning.

Lyle opened his eyes, still disoriented and with his head still swimming, but quickly gathering his bearings. Mother was already out of her Nest and standing over him, waiting for him. That only made Lyle want to take his time.

But he also wanted to get this over with.

He stepped out of the Nest and looked around the room, noting the difference between what he had been raised with and what he had made for himself. Mother's Roost was filled with top-of-the-line gear. Four Nests: one calibrated for her, the other for Lyle, and a pair for use by close family and friends.

"What the hell were you thinking?" Mother asked without preamble.

"I was thinking about going out on my own," Lyle responded in his calmest voice. "And that it was finally time for me to make something for myself."

"You've *been* making something for yourself!" Mother was already yelling. "And now you're ruining it — destroying the brand I've spent the last two decades building."

"I don't see it that way," Lyle said, still calm and shaking his head.

"And how do *you* see it?" Mother snarled.

"As a new product line that you don't have to manage."

"Oh, you've got this one, do you?"

"Yes." Lyle smiled at the edges of his victory. "I absolutely do."

"What makes you think you're ready to manage

anything?"

"Only a lifetime of experience."

"The only experience you have is in doing exactly what you're told."

"Exactly," Lyle agreed.

"You're not ready to be in charge of anything."

"And yet, I'm done with being your puppet, so here we are."

Mother looked slapped, had to blink twice before she could conjure an answer. "You're not my puppet, Lyle. You're my partner."

"I'm your underling and we both know it. The only voice I'm allowed to have is the one you've given me. You want to keep me a little boy forever. I'm only seen as your child, instead of as a man of my own." He shook his head, more emphatic. "I'm not doing it anymore."

"You have no idea what you've done."

"And what have I done, Mother? Please, tell me."

"You've brought your poisonous snake of a father back into our lives. That man can't be trusted!"

"Maybe he can't." Lyle looked at her evenly. "Can you?"

"What's that supposed to mean?"

"He accused you of some pretty heinous shit."

"And you believe him?"

"Why don't you give me a reason not to," Lyle said.

"Why should I dignify his bullshit with any response?" Then: "What did he say?"

"That you poisoned him with Estravir, and that the drug led to a loss of impulse control, reduced executive function and mental health issues. Apparently, you poisoning my father sent him into an institution and led to a degenerative condition with his brain."

"Are you really questioning me right now?"

"I am. Are you really incapable of answering me?"

"You already know the answer. Your father is a lying piece of shit who abandoned us and is now stomping back into our lives with the same crap he left us with twenty years ago. How dare you—"

"Question you?"

Mother stared without replying.

Lyle's only choice was to let his hate boil. He had been onto her game for a while now and had never seen her more clearly.

The principles she taught as part of Ruthlessly Positive were just this same ugly manipulation wearing the lipstick of slippery language. The last thing Lyle wanted was to feel sympathy for the man who had abandoned him — twenty years was too long, regardless of what had happened to him.

And yet, Lyle could also imagine what it might have been like for his father to be poisoned, and for that venom to erode his mental capacity, and maybe even slowly remold his personality.

"Yes," she finally answered. "How dare you question me, after all I've done for you."

"And what exactly have you done for me?"

"I've made you rich, or haven't you—"

"You made yourself rich. I've been getting the same amount each week now for more than five years."

"And that's not good enough for you? How about this house and the cars and the clothes and the trips and the—"

"I don't give a shit about any of it!" Lyle screamed.

And truly he didn't.

The only thing he wanted right now, the only thing he cared about in this very second, was getting free of his mother so he could eventually go his own way.

"Then what do you care about, Lyle?"

"I want my trust."

She laughed. "What makes you think you're ready to handle that kind of money?"

"It shouldn't matter whether I can handle it or not. *I earned it.* And if you can't trust me enough to run my own arm of the business when I'm already an adult, then it really is time for me to go off on my own."

"You're just like your father," she said, grabbing a guilt trip to tighten her noose. "I've spent the most important years of my life trying to help you overcome the negative tendencies you inherited from that man."

She shook her head in mourning, disappointed by the world and her son and most of all herself — that's what she wanted Lyle to believe right now in this thoroughly broken moment. "But I've clearly failed you. It's a shame how little you understand."

"And what is it that I'm too dim to comprehend, Mother?"

"That you'll never be more than a failure without me."

"Are you worried about me, or that I might make you look bad? You know what?" Lyle shook his head. "I don't even give a shit. I'm done with this."

Then he marched out of the room without looking back.

On the other side of the door he pulled out his phone and started typing.

I'm sorry you're sick. But I need to see you. Can we meet somewhere, now — in real life?

Lyle felt ruthless toward his mother, but barely positive about anything.

He stared at the screen, waiting for Kam to message him back, sure he was about to read a *NO!*

But instead, he got something even worse.

Chapter Ten

Kam

KAM WASN'T JUST PANICKING, her entire body was pimpled in hives, even now, two hours after she got the message from Lyle which she was still ignoring.

She was drenched in sweat and she could taste something foul, like rotting meat in her molars. It was only her imagination, but here in the real world thoughts were unrelenting demons, unwilling to surrender and give her so much as a moment's reprieve.

Kam couldn't stand the thought of Lyle seeing her. Not here outside eScape, where instead of staring into the eyes of an avatar she had spent 327 hours designing, he would see her dying body. He would know how poor she really was. Worse than underprivileged or impoverished, Kam was flat-out destitute. A human disease who wasn't deserving of the little life she had left. An obvious thief who had burgled a better reality by way of brute force hacking. Taking what wasn't hers so she could pretend to belong with the world's elite.

But the truth was she lived at the bottom and that's where she would die, in a squalid hovel in the rundowns.

Lyle would never want to see her if he knew the truth, in eScape or out here in the real world, fetid and decaying as her corner most certainly was.

She looked at his last message again, but it still hadn't changed.

I'm sorry you're sick. But I need to see you. Can we meet somewhere, now — in real life?

Kam finally answered: *Sure! My friend Raquel is having a party tonight. Sort of an after-party after-party to celebrate your event today. You want to meet there?*

The entire party would be a disguise she could wear to hide how pathetic she really was.

Sounds great. Message me the address.

It's in eScape, she wrote. *Is that okay?*

If you'll be there, then YES!

That was easier than Kam had imagined. She wondered how many times she could get away with a maneuver like that. Maybe she shouldn't have invited him. It was only a matter of time before the situation folded back on itself and Lyle learned that the girl he might like was really a fraud.

But she couldn't afford to worry about that. So Kam messaged the address and then barred herself from considering the worst of it. Her secret was safe for now and that would have to be enough.

She messaged Raquel, saying she changed her mind and would be coming to the party after all. Things had fallen through with Chad, but no worries, she'd met another guy named Jaxon and would be bringing him along.

Only then did Kam realize how much she wished that Lyle could attend the party as himself. Even if she couldn't, and even as much as she hated Ruthless Positivity, her friends were all obsessed, and it would have been legendary, her showing up at Raquel's party with Lyle Grace on her arm.

Kam could imagine all the wide-open mouths and involuntary staring as the pair of them sauntered through the room. And she liked what she saw.

But that was only her ego talking. The reality would be awful. Except for the handful of lottery winners Raquel had invited to the party, just about everyone else would be fans or perhaps even clients. A celebrity to that particular crowd, Lyle would be mobbed and Kam would barely see him.

It was better this way, even if she had to live without the glory.

LYLE WAS ALREADY WAITING when she got there.

His body belonged to Jaxon, but she'd been looking into those eyes for her entire life.

"It's good to see you." He took her hand. "I've been thinking about you all day."

"I've been thinking about you, too," Kam admitted.

That little lightning strike in her heart was back, reminding her that this was all temporary, and that she didn't deserve the little she had.

Lyle replied with a wide smile and offered his hand.

She slipped hers inside it, then together they entered the party.

Looking around, she didn't see Raquel or Dee or Kelso, and she barely knew anyone else. She'd only been friends with the group for a few months, after Pibly homed in on the trio as a potential entry into Lyle's inner circle, thanks to their shared number of touch points, both with each other, and with Ruthlessly Positive.

"Do you know all of these people?" He sounded slightly overwhelmed, a surprising thought considering his life's usual bedlam.

"Not really," Kam answered, feeling lost.

"Shall we find your friends?"

"We shall," she said with a smile and a squeeze of his hand.

Through the living room, parlor, and kitchen, then out back to the grotto, around the sweeping lawn to the small theater, and back inside by way of the game room, where an obvious lottery winner was standing alone, gulping down what looked like a tall glass of whisky.

Still no friends in sight, so Kam led Lyle upstairs to Raquel's spa. Sure enough, there they were. All three of them, ready to get undressed for the sauna.

"Care to join us?" Kelso asked as they entered.

"Who's your friend?" Raquel asked, clearly liking what she saw.

"Jaxon," he said, extending his hand.

Dee was the first to shake it, introducing herself as she did. Then Kelso, followed by Raquel.

"What are you guys doing up here?" Kam asked.

"Raquel is over it," Kelso told her.

"I'm not sure I was ever really under it," Raquel laughed.

"This is your party?" Lyle asked.

"Sure is," Raquel said.

"Then why have it, if you were *never really under it?*"

"Because," Raquel replied, clearly not appreciating Lyle's question. "My parents like to throw as many parties as possible. It gets their names in circulation. I like to help them out."

"So this is their party?" Lyle tried to clarify.

"It's their *house*. Do you have a point?"

"Not at all, just curious. Forgive me for—"

There was a deafening boom from downstairs.

"What was that?" Kelso and Dee both spoke at once, as the group turned toward the door.

Raquel was already walking toward it.

Everyone followed.

Downstairs and into the game room — ground zero for the commotion.

It was the lottery winner, swaying on his feet with a cackle. The crowd watched as he slowly recovered his balance, walked over and picked up the nearest chair, then heaved it over his head and hurled it against the wall.

It shattered into pieces and sent two of the chair's legs skittering across the Spanish tile floor, over to the broken corpse of the first fallen chair.

The lottery winner bellowed with laughter.

Raquel yelled at her AI to hurry the hell up and get the eScape police. They entered the room a beat later. She didn't even wait for them to leave, and speaking too loudly as they escorted the winner out of the room, Raquel said, "Lottery loser's more like it."

She laughed, then so did Kelso and Dee.

Lyle looked at Kam and she gave him a shrug no one else bothered to see.

"Who was that?" Lyle asked.

"Some dude who won the lottery in the real world and spent a shit ton of credits in here. He lives in Elysium, and built a fucking pyramid at the end of his cul-de-sac. My parents said I'm not allowed to throw a party without inviting the guy. I'm supposed to be nice, but that's the second time he's been kicked out."

"Maybe that's because everyone is always picking on him," Kam suggested, surprising herself.

Raquel looked over, equally shocked. "It's because he's too white trash to even turn off his drinking filters. Getting drunk in eScape is a choice."

Kam surprised herself again. "Maybe it's how he deals with no one being nice to him."

"You've gotta be kidding me right now." Raquel snorted. "Lottery winners are the *worst*. They shouldn't even be here. They stink up eScape's best neighborhoods with their new-money bullshit."

"She's right," Dee agreed. "Their assumptions are insulting."

Kelso nodded along. "Winning a bunch of money doesn't make you a winner in life. Those people don't know how to spend their credits because they've never had to earn any of them."

"Have you?" Lyle asked, keeping his voice pleasant.

"The crass enthusiasm for showing off their new non-wealth, that will surely be gone in no time since it was never supposed to be theirs to begin with, it's …"

"Threatening?" Lyle tried to finish.

"*Annoying*," Raquel said, still glaring at him. "And what is it you think *I'd* be threatened about? Did you not hear me that he built a pyramid?"

"It's a whole Egyptian theme," Kelso added.

"Instead of lawn gnomes and pink flamingoes, he has a giant sphinx and like a thousand weird-looking statues." Dee wrinkled her nose in disgust.

"*Ooh, threatening.*" Raquel laughed. "You know that asshole has a bunch of virtual exotic pets that keep escaping his pyramid and wandering all around Elysium?"

"Does that directly affect you?" Lyle asked, seeming almost comically concerned.

"I heard he eats ground beef," Kelso said.

Dee looked horrified.

"Where do *you* live, New Guy?" Raquel asked Lyle. "You seem awfully interested in defending the proletariat."

"I'm just trying to understand what's making you feel so threatened."

"I'm not threatened!" Raquel scoffed.

"You just think lottery winners shouldn't be allowed to live in your neighborhood, even if they can afford it?"

Raquel spoke without breaking her stare. "No, Jaxon, I don't think that lottery winners should be sharing the same neighborhoods with families who earned their fortunes a long time ago. They can enjoy whatever they want to, I don't give a shit, but they should stick to the parts of this place that are open to everyone. They can blow their credits on all the experiences they want, but they shouldn't have exclusive access when they haven't earned their place."

"My mom says that most of us wouldn't have bought into Elysium if we'd known they'd end opening the neighborhood to just anyone," Dee added.

"I don't know ..." Kelso said, and for a second it seemed like he was close to saying something kind, instead of condescending. "It really isn't their fault, being born poor and all. Imagine if we couldn't feed our doggies Wagyu? They would probably eat from a can without even realizing that's all just lips and assholes."

Dee nodded. "Kelso has a point. But even old dogs can learn new tricks if you get the right trainer. Do you guys know Jessup Toley?"

No one responded.

"It doesn't matter. He works with a guy who does jobs

for my dad. He won the lottery like thirty years ago, and he eventually learned how to behave."

"Exactly," Kelso agreed with Dee. "They just need to be taught how to act in a civilized way."

"Fine," Raquel said. "They can find their own neighborhoods until they do."

"So, I think I've got this …" Lyle started, after the silence had settled. "Lottery winners are like dogs who need to be housebroken, and the guy who just got escorted out of here is like a dog that's flunked out of obedience training. So, my question is, *does this apply to just lottery winners, or all people who made their money fast?*"

"Are you being sarcastic?" Raquel asked.

Dee was more direct. "Who the hell do you think you are?"

Then Kelso to Kam: "Who the hell does he think he is? Sounds like New Money."

She had been getting angrier and angrier, but now Kam was long beyond mortified. She had introduced these people as her friends, but they were an embarrassment. Lyle seemed to be taking it all in good humor, but Kam wasn't feeling nearly as generous. She wanted to strangle all three of them, and maybe do worse to Raquel. She was worried about answering, or opening her mouth at all. One wrong word would tip into another, and soon she'd be screaming a flurry of insults she could never take back. Then her reputation would be ruined.

She swallowed, then opened her mouth.

Lyle saved her before she spoke. "We've all had different backgrounds, but it's safe to say that everyone here might have a skewed perspective. I know that I've always had enough, so I can't have any idea what it would feel like to live in abject poverty." He pointed to his chest, then gestured around. "I grew up in places like this. I'm spoiled. Aren't all of us?"

"Only the good kind," Kelso laughed.

Then Raquel and Dee joined him.

Lyle came last, but his laughter was the loudest.

Maybe he was trying to cover for her desert of mirth, but that didn't smother her fury. There were so many things she wanted to say, but Kam couldn't get a single one of them out of her mouth.

She had to hold them all inside.

And that made her avatar glitch.

Lyle was the only one who noticed, but his reaction was dramatic, flinching wide eyes and a full turn of his body. He leaned toward her with a whisper. "Are you okay?"

"I'm fine," she lied.

Lyle held Kam by the arms and looked into her eyes.

"Come with me," he said.

Chapter Eleven

Lyle

"You have to promise me that you'll never tell anyone what you're about to see."

"What am I going to see?" Kam asked, the wonder clear on her face.

"*Promise me*," Lyle repeated.

She drew a breath, looked up into his eyes, and parted her lips with a whisper. "I promise."

"What do you promise?" Lyle smiled; now he was just having fun.

"I promise that I'll never ever tell anyone what you're about to show me ... *no matter what.*"

Lyle liked that last part a lot. He took Kam's hand and led her out of the party, then into a warp room where they instantly vanished in one place only to reappear in another. Specifically, in front of the small apartment he kept inside eScape.

"It looks just like I imagined it would," Kam said as she stepped through the door.

"And how is that?"

"Like the real you, instead of the one you play for your mom."

Lyle likely looked wounded, but he was feeling something else.

"What is this place?" Kam asked as Lyle closed the door behind them.

"A surprise," Lyle replied with a smile.

He had spent a lot on this room, but it was worth every credit. Privacy-enforced, with permissions set to keep the world out, and anyone from monitoring what happened inside.

The place was made to look like his childhood. Set up as a small seminar space, the kind of place where he and Mother worked in the early years of Ruthless Positivity. Before her program became a household name and Julia Grace personally consulted some of the biggest names in the world, including two prime ministers and a president.

Back in the early days Lyle was desperate to be a good boy. But according to Mother, her son's worst self kept getting in the way. Over and over he kept causing problems, and she kept having to fix them. He didn't want to cause all those issues, and it withered his insides to know he was, but there was little Lyle could do beyond trying harder, listening better, and doing his best to be the good boy that both he and his mommy knew he could be.

"I don't like this place." Kam glanced around, shaking her head, looking and sounding uncertain.

"Do you trust me?"

She stopped and looked at him, then without hesitation said, "I do."

He took her hands, squeezed, then let them go with a smile. He pulled out his phone and ordered it to do something with dancing fingers.

The seminar space expanded around them, getting fuller rather than bigger, suddenly populated by row upon row of dummy avatars.

The new crowd did nothing to soothe her. She took a decisive step back, more uncertain than ever.

"It's okay," Lyle promised.

"What is this place?"

"They're dummies."

"Clearly, if they're here for Ruthless Positivity."

They both laughed.

"They're programmed to react with enthusiasm to whatever you want to say."

Kam still looked confused, but curiosity had also nested inside her expression. There was a sly smile as she asked how it worked.

But Lyle didn't want to tell her, preferring to show her instead.

Again he took her hand, but this time he led her to the dais overlooking the room.

He stood behind it. Kam's uncertainty had bloomed into a breed of bewilderment, her lips back and eyes forward, ready to see or hear or experience whatever Lyle wanted to show her.

"I have met puddles deeper than your friend Raquel," he bellowed from behind the podium.

Kam blurted laughter, clearly caught off guard. But then she really lost her shit when all the dummy avatars began to whoop and holler and applaud with audible *amen!s*.

"Your turn," he said.

Now Kam was beaming. She drew a breath and yelled, "I'm tired of being looked down on for something that isn't my fault!"

The audience erupted in applause. Molten lava

affection.

"I'm sick of always feeling disappointed! Of being punished for who I am! For expecting so little out of life and still getting even less than that!"

The crowd continued to explode with a Big Bang of positive energy.

Kam's body was glowing, as if her entire self had been drenched in a halo. For a moment she looked deeply, truly happy. Rapture made her stunning. Lyle could feel something there, like a cold wind blowing into a warm house.

"It feels good, doesn't it?"

"Amazing," Kam answered from behind the purest of smiles.

"Do it again," Lyle invited.

So she did. And he followed.

They traded turns for an hour, each of them expressing their unacceptable emotions, bellowing at the top of their lungs, pulling from a long list of times when they had to pretend that everything was fine even though it was all so very obviously not.

Their grievances started out long, like when Kam screamed, "You could never ever admit when you were wrong and I hated you so much for that! You were always correcting me for everything, no matter how hard I tried or what I did! You never failed to tell me when I was wrong, but never even once admitted when you were!"

She stopped for a breath as the avatars brayed with laughter, cheering her on.

But by the end both of their shouts had turned into the simplest of interchangeable statements, passed like trading cards between them. The only difference lay in the tense.

I hate how you never asked for my opinion!
I can't stand that you're never really honest!
You always dismissed my feeling by calling me moody!

I hate how much my own father never really knew his daughter at all!

And the crowd kept erupting in cheers, rolling through swelling waves of raucous laughter.

The mini-confessions continued to escalate, until Kam suddenly burst out with something Lyle wasn't sure she really meant to say. That was the danger of this room; he'd done it plenty of times himself.

"I think I hate my father!"

The audience applauded as Kam clapped a hand over her mouth and burst into tears.

"It's okay," Lyle said, pulling her against him.

She sobbed against his chest. A heavy cry, he could feel her tears soaking through his shirt.

"It's okay," he repeated.

But still she sobbed harder.

The crowd thought it was all a little too hilarious, so Lyle had to turn them down a bit before shutting them off entirely. They disappeared, then a few seconds later Kam was finally finished collecting herself.

She wiped her eyes and said, "Sorry."

"You have nothing to be sorry about," he promised. "Do you want to talk about it?"

She nodded. "No."

Lyle laughed. "Take your time."

"My dad is dead."

"Should I be sorry to hear that? Or did you need some applause? Did I turn off our cheering section too soon?"

Kam laughed back, wiping at her eyes again. "It's my fault. That he's dead, I mean."

"I'm sure that's not true unless this is the part where you tell me you're really a murderer."

"Well, not a murderer in the way you're thinking, but he'd be alive right now if I'd stopped him from leaving the house. He was having one of his hallucinations. It had happened plenty of times, but I knew how to pull him out of it and make him take his meds. I just didn't want to. I was sick of doing it, and even sicker of never being appreciated for having to in the first place. My father always resented it, and sometimes he hit me."

Kam wiped another tear. "So he left the house tripping and walked in front of a bus. That sure sounds like my fault to me."

"Sounds like it would have happened sooner without you around."

That got Kam crying even harder, and Lyle wasn't sure if that was a good thing or not.

She wiped her eyes again, collected her breath, and said, "Do you think I'm a bad person?"

Lyle laughed without meaning to. "Of course not."

"Then why are you laughing at me?"

"Because you asked such a ridiculous question." He nodded toward the front row of empty chairs. "Wanna sit with me?"

"Sure," she smiled.

Seconds later they were both in their chairs, and Lyle was starting on his story.

"You should never feel bad about being a human, and in case you didn't know it, everyone wants to kill their parents at least once or twice. So not only are you normal, you're actually an over-achiever." He winked. "You should really be proud of yourself."

A twitter of laughter, then, "Thanks. I'll remember that."

"Seriously, I feel that way about my mom sometimes. Everyone thinks we have such a great relationship, but I hate her so much sometimes."

"I know," Kam said.

He looked at her. "How do you know?"

"Are you kidding?" She laughed. "Who else were you just screaming at?"

"Oh. Right." Lyle gave her a sheepish grin. "Wanna hear a story?"

"Of course."

"Once upon a time my mom was a bitch and your dad was an asshole."

Kam laughed, harder this time.

Lyle continued. "Seriously, when I was around seven years old or so I made a friend named Sebastian. We met at one of her camps, but he didn't know who I was. I'd never had so much fun in my life. We played all the time. Simple stuff, like hide-and-seek. But I never got to hang out with kids my own age, so it was a really big deal. My mom put a stop to it, though. There's a lot of awful shit she did during my childhood and this is far from the worst of it, but I still think about it all the time."

"What happened?"

"It's not going to sound like a big deal …"

"Just say it."

"I wanted to hang out with Sebastian one day and she wasn't even doing anything. So I asked if we could play hide-and-seek or something. She didn't say no, it might have been better if she had. Instead, Mother asked why I wanted to spend time with Sebastian instead of her, like she was in competition with him. I'd never thought about it like that, and tried to explain that I only wanted to play. Of course I still loved her. But she kept going on and on about it until I finally told Sebastian that we couldn't be friends anymore. When I brought it up later, Mother told me that I'd misunderstood what she wanted. But I hadn't. The more I've played the exchange in my head over the years, the more I understand *exactly* what happened. Mother's always wanted my social life to include her, and she's always expected me to prioritize our relationship over everything else."

Kam was listening, though it looked like she might have plenty to say.

Lyle continued. "She never had her own friends or support network. It was just her clients, and fans, and me. But guess who had to fulfill all her needs? It was enough for me to be *her* best friend, she didn't really ever care enough about my needs to realize that she could never be mine. So yeah …" Lyle sighed. "My mom's controlling behavior has always been borderline abusive, and there were plenty of times when I wished she was dead."

"At least you never acted on it," Kam said.

"How do you know I haven't tried?"

Her smile split into another light laugh, then they fell into a mutual quiet.

Lyle had never had the chance to bond with someone like this, not about his true feelings. It felt remarkable to admit that he'd never felt the way he was "supposed to," and Lyle was sure she was feeling something similar, if not the same damned thing.

"Why do you need this room?" Kam finally asked.

Lyle looked at her, confused. Hadn't he just shown her?

"I mean, wouldn't it be better if you could just really say what you feel all the time?"

"Because," Lyle said, feeling another person's words on his lips, "white lies are sometimes necessary, no matter how you might feel about them. Think about how much chaos there would be if people stopped being positive."

And yet, for the first time in his life, Lyle knew that wasn't true, and could feel it on a cellular level. Not just the lie, but the desire behind it.

He wouldn't mind a little chaos. Not at all.

So he leaned in and kissed her.
Kam kissed him back.
And Lyle knew what Heaven tasted like.

Chapter Twelve

Kam

KAM COULDN'T BELIEVE they were kissing.

She had never felt anything even close to this.

And she never saw it coming, but Kam did *feel it*, a split-second before his lips were on hers, insistent and unyielding. Lyle wrapped his arms around Kam and pulled her against his chest.

She buried her hands in his hair, just like she'd wanted to do ever since that afternoon spent skipping through The Palisades together.

Brown hair curled around her fingers. Beating wings in her heart and her head and her stomach. This was as close to Heaven as Kam had ever come, and she would give anything to keep it from ending.

Lyle kissed her harder as she sighed into it; her body was soft, but still ultimately digital, allowing her to do and feel so much more inside eScape than she could have ever imagined experiencing outside of it.

She pulled away, needing to say something out loud, verify that this impossible moment was real.

But he pulled her back the second she did, and for Kam that was more than enough. The truth was fixed to her face, and swimming in her mouth.

Kam Landry really was kissing Lyle Grace.

And she never, ever wanted him to stop.

Kam had been dreaming about this moment for much longer than she was willing to admit. Her fantasies were stupid and childish, just like the rest of her. Proof that she couldn't grow up. But Kam couldn't help it; she felt a kinship with Lyle, like his mother was somehow her mother, too. Ever since their first meeting — when he was six and she was nine, not that Lyle would ever remember — Kam could see how miserable he was, living under his mother's thumb like he was.

No one else seemed to understand what they were seeing. But Kam's experience gave her a sort of X-ray vision. She went from seeing Lyle as a little brother, to fantasizing that he would one day do to her exactly what he was doing now.

The anger was still there, bubbling under the surface. But at least now she knew where it was coming from and could keep the emotions sequestered where they belonged. She wasn't mad at Lyle for making up with his father, or for putting on a show. He was doing what he needed to, and if she could accept it, then maybe he was even doing it partly for her.

She sure wanted to believe that, and part of her *needed* to.

It was time for Lyle to do something on his own; Kam couldn't disagree, she'd been thinking the same thing forever.

She had to stop fixing her perspective to Lyle's. Kam's relationship with—

"Are you okay?" Lyle asked, pulling away.

"Of course … I'm … *happy*."

Lyle smiled, seeming relieved. "You seem so far away."

Kam leaned in and kissed him again, willing her mind away from its usual loops.

Her father was the last thing she wanted to think about right now, but he was a cancer of images and emotions. She could see him standing over her with a scowl, could hear his barrage of belittling insults, and feel the unsettling temperature of his predictably unpredictable ire.

Even while kissing the man of her dreams, Kam couldn't escape the haunting of her thoughts. They didn't belong in this moment, and yet memories and images were like toilet paper on her heel, broadcasting embarrassment behind her.

While Lyle was patching things up with his father, Kam couldn't stop thinking about the day hers died. Instead of the guilt she expected, she felt only a numb relief that she was finally free. Kam applied for early emancipation and welfare support when the foster care system tried to place her in a home, and had been living on her own ever since.

At first she was happy. Being by herself was paradise, compared to living with her father. But by her 18th birthday Kam was too weak to leave the house. That's when she started studying with XzO, a fellow hacker she met online. The plan was clear, even if back then Kam wasn't sure she would ever be able to pull off the impossible — escaping her physical body and living forever inside eScape.

She could never earn enough credits to buy her way in legitimately, not before her body finally quit on her. And the lotteries were bullshit. Even winners were looked down on. She hated liars, and yet Kam would have to lie her way inside if she didn't want to die.

The shame felt like a stain on her psyche as she tried to lose herself in the moment.

But Kam was too close to him. His issues had become her issues. Her only thoughts right now should be his lips on hers, her hands on his skin, two bodies pressing together.

But Kam was ruminating, only half with Lyle, even though she was willing to offer him all of herself. Instead of being present, she was somewhere far off, thinking about how she had never dealt with the erratic behavior and emotional abuse that kept her trapped in a psychological closet; at her body for developing a crippling disease that was doing everything it could to kill her early; at Lyle's mom for inventing all the bullshit she was fed throughout her childhood about negative thoughts and emotions being poison for the soul, and that saying the positive opposite is the way to cleanse — or suppress — them.

Lyle pulled away again, but it somehow seemed like he was closer to Kam than ever. He stared into her eyes, and she could swear that their hearts were beating in time.

"You're a really good kisser."

Kam could feel herself blushing. She gave him the slightest shake of her head. "No …"

"Really, I mean it. You're so …"

She didn't wait for him to finish. Kam kissed him again, this time without any thoughts of what should be. No thoughts of her father or his. Julia Grace was finally out of her head, and so was everyone else.

For the first time the moment was theirs. And Lyle belonged to her.

Kam mashed her lips against his, now the aggressor. She kept going until she needed a breath.

She pulled away from him, panting. "I've never done this before …"

He opened his mouth to respond, but that seemed to arouse Lyle even more than he already was. He was on her in a blink.

"I have, but not like this."

"What do you mean?" Kam asked, pulling away again, hating herself for asking what was probably a stupid question, but needing to know the answer anyway.

He laughed, and the sound seemed to surprise him. A sigh, then, "I've had a couple of one-night stands, but they didn't mean anything. It was only to see what I could get away with behind Mother's back. I never knew it could feel so …"

"Real?" she finished.

"Real," he agreed.

Then they were back to kissing.

Kam was euphoric. Happier than she had ever felt. She'd confessed to one of her biggest secrets: that she was new and inexperienced and entirely in his hands. Lyle hadn't just accepted that, he seemed to appreciate her admission.

A weight had been lifted from her body. No, from her soul. A burden Kam had been dragging behind her for a lifetime. At least *her* lifetime. There were no new epiphanies as they kissed. Only old feelings she was finally willing to acknowledge.

Kam was in love with him.

What felt like a possibility before now had the tone of irrefutable truth. She just had to admit it: *Yes, she was in love with Lyle.* Because he understood her in a way that no one else ever had, or could.

And she gave the same to him. She always had, though now he could finally know.

It was an onslaught of emotions. Too many coming at once. Kam had no way to escape, nor did she want to. Instead, she longed to understand what she was feeling. A sensation that seemed to permeate every pore of her body. Arousal and catharsis, pure and undiluted excitement.

She had never felt like this and was suddenly worried she might never feel this way again.

There was something beyond the arousal, insistent and pressing against her. Perhaps her failing body was becoming less able to withstand the strain of being in a Deep Spell.

Just a few days ago, Kam wondered if she would die before having sex, and had even considered paying for it inside eScape. She was glad that she hadn't, but now she needed to hurry up and give her body what it was begging for.

What she knew Lyle's body wanted, too.

She pulled away again, but this time it was to take off her top.

Kam pictured her virtual blouse in a puddle on the floor, next to her skirt and panties. But Lyle raised a hand to stop her.

"You don't want to?" Kam asked, her heart splitting down the center with rejection.

"Of course I do. Just not here."

"Oh," she smiled. "Where do you want to … you know?"

"At the Hotel Bisou."

"Oh!" Kam actually giggled.

If the Hotel Bisou wasn't the most exclusive hotel inside eScape, it was for sure at the top of the list. Kam wasn't sure how much longer she had before her body threatened to quit and yanked her out of this place, but looking into Lyle's eyes right now it was impossible to refuse him.

"I want our first time to be special."

"Our first time," she repeated, tasting the words. "That sounds nice."

"I'll be right back."

Lyle didn't wait for a response. He vanished, then reappeared a few seconds later as Lyle. "I had to log out. The Hotel Bisou would never let us in if I was wearing the anonymous avatar."

"Oh …" she said again, though that wasn't what Kam was thinking at all.

She was thinking, *I'm about to be seen in public with the real-life Lyle Grace.*

And as exciting a thought as that was, Kam couldn't shake the unmistakable sense that felt too much like a fact.

Something was about to go terribly wrong, and there was nothing she could do to change that.

Chapter Thirteen

Lyle

LYLE HAD EXACTLY ONE OBJECTIVE: to reach the Hotel Bisou without being seen.

He could have logged out when they got there, but that didn't feel right. Last thing he wanted to do was insult Kam in any way, and declaring her on his arm was the best way to make her feel heard and seen and understood — all obviously things she had been living too much of her life without.

Even if Mother's Ruthless Positivity was largely bull-shit, she managed to amass the millions of fans she had thanks to the kernel of truth in everything she did. A life-time around her business made Lyle able to recognize some of those same patterns himself. And right now, Kam wanted the same thing as him. To hold hands like a real couple, converse without worry, and enjoy each other's company, free from judgements, schedules, or sabotage.

Conversation was fluid, without any pauses. They

could have gone into any warp booth and ended up in front of the hotel, and they'd even considered doing so. But neither of them wanted to break the spell, and a long walk from one corner of eScape to another, with a few well-placed shortcuts, felt like the perfect way to get acquainted. And cool down before heating up atop the hotel's luxurious sheets.

Lyle had been with girls before, but not like this. The anticipation was almost a physical ache, so he kept himself from thinking about it, and did his best to stay present in their conversation. The rules were simple: they could ask each other anything, but they each had to answer every question asked. That mandate had so far kept the queries shallow.

"What's something that makes you laugh out loud?" Kam had asked.

And Lyle had said, "Believe it or not, dad jokes."

"You've gotta be kidding me."

"Nope." He shook his head and squeezed her hand. "I know they're stupid, but maybe it's because I grew up without a father around. Either way, I think dad jokes are *hilarious*."

"Do you have a favorite?"

"Like fifty."

"Care to share one?"

Lyle turned to look at Kam; her eyes said she meant it. After a second of thought, he said, "If a child refuses to take a nap, then does that mean they're guilty of resisting a rest?"

No response.

"Oh come on, that's funny."

"*Maybe*," she said. "If you've never heard a joke before."

Lyle laughed, shaking his head as they walked. "I feel sorry for your lack of culture. You don't even know a good dad joke when you hear it."

"What is it that makes for a 'good' dad joke?"

"Well, first off, the joke has to be bad. And by bad I mean both corny and kind of amusing. Puns are especially golden."

"Do the jokes have to be delivered by a dad?" Kam asked.

"Oh, absolutely. Otherwise it's probably just a really bad joke."

"So what you just said, about resisting arrest, that's not a dad joke."

"That's definitely a dad joke."

"But you're not a dad … are you?"

A light laugh. "No. Not yet. But I did hear that one from a dad at one of our seminars. That's where I've heard almost all of my dad jokes. Usually from fathers intentionally trying to embarrass their children."

"My dad never bothered with jokes. He embarrassed me by saying I was worthless instead."

"I'm sorry." He squeezed her hand again.

"Don't be. That was a joke."

"He didn't call you worthless?"

"Oh, he totally did. But it's the truth in it that makes it funny."

"So, okay, abusive dad insults aside, what makes you laugh out loud?"

"Do you want something actually funny? Or can it be stupid like dad jokes?"

"Definitely stupid."

"Okay then," she laughed. "Videos where animals are doing stupid things always make me laugh."

"Stupid things like what?"

"Have you seen the one where that tiny little dog and that big giant dog are barking at one another?"

"Seriously?" Lyle said. "You'll need to be more specific."

Kam laughed again. "I think it's a chihuahua and a Great Dane or a mastiff or something. The chihuahua is just yapping and yapping and yapping at him. The big dog is just sort of ignoring him, but every once in a while he makes a really loud bark. Then the tiny dog cowers back for a second before launching himself forward, yapping even louder than he was before."

"Sounds *hilarious*."

"Shut up," Kam said. "It's really funny."

"How do you spend your mornings?" Lyle asked.

It seemed like an innocent question, but Kam's answers would reveal plenty. Did she wake up and get going with her day immediately, or lounge around, thinking or reading or meditating in a room by herself? Did she exercise, shower, make breakfast for herself?

Lyle was dying to know every little thing about her.

"I hope you're not looking for an answer better than, *I spend an hour or so hating the day before I get out of bed wanting to punch it in the face,* because that's all I have."

He grinned. "Good enough for me."

"What about you?"

"Ugh, I don't want to talk about it."

"Then you shouldn't have asked the question."

"Fair enough." Lyle shrugged, still walking. "Mother makes me practice for our upcoming broadcast, whatever it might be. The same thing every morning, and I always hate it. You were right, I shouldn't have asked."

"Do you keep in touch with your childhood friends?" Kam asked.

"Not to sound like a sad sack, but I never really had any."

"Me neither," she admitted. "What's the last book you read?"

"I've been reading a book about anti-gravity. It's impossible to put down."

A beat of silence followed by what sounded like an accidental laugh. "Is that a dad joke?"

"Do you want it to be?"

"Well," she said, "You're not a dad."

"I'm a proud member of Ruthless Positivity, so there's no way I'm letting that stop me. Check it out: *Why can't you hear a pterodactyl go to the bathroom?*"

Kam laughed. "Why?"

"Because the pee is silent."

"You really need to stop now."

They kept walking and laughing and talking.

This was what Lyle had always wanted but so far in his life had witnessed in shadows, and felt only as a brush against his skin from something beautiful but out of reach and always edging away. He'd watched it on-screen and read it on the page, but Lyle had slowly come to believe that he could never be loved for him, and that's why Jaxon was born.

This felt so different than anything Lyle had ever experienced. Women had constantly thrown themselves at him, from adolescence on. But Mother always told him that they would only want his money. He hated to believe it, and admitting the truth even more, but so far that truth had been impossible to argue with. No one gave a shit about who he really was. Interactions with the opposite sex always made Lyle feel like the other person could only see him through their own lens, wanting to know how he reflected back on them.

But that wasn't true with Kam. There was nothing performative about their exchanges, though of course he wanted to impress her, and was trying his hardest without really trying.

Lyle had been craving a normal life where he didn't always have to perform. Mother wouldn't allow it. He was her employee, even if she wouldn't admit it. And until his 21st birthday, she controlled all of his money, and most of his decisions. But he knew by now, she wouldn't turn it over even then. He would have to get a lawyer, and things would get ugly.

He'd been dreaming of a split with Mother, and had his reasons for a while. Holding Kam's hand a few blocks from the Hotel Bisou, those reasons now felt irrefutable.

Her acidic behavior was holding him back. Mother was fond of saying "that no girl his age could ever love him as much as she does."

When Lyle was little, her words were like a warm blanket when it was snowing outside. Mother was enough for him then. But she still saw him as a little boy who didn't know any better. And she wanted to keep him there, no matter how unhealthy it was. The more Lyle tried to pull away, the more she dug her claws into his psyche.

Lyle had been longing to leave for a while, but deep down he knew escape was impossible. Yes, he resented her controlling nature, understood its toxicity on an instinctive level, and prayed for a way out, back when he thought someone might answer those prayers. But it didn't matter how much he might resent her, leaving would make him the same strain of asshole as his father.

"What are you thinking about?" Kam asked.

They were rounding the corner. In another block and a half they would reach the hotel. So in addition to daydreaming about his upcoming separation from Mother, Lyle was also imagining Kam slipping her blouse over her head, stepping out of her skirt and panties, then climbing onto the bed.

He pictured kissing her, pushing himself into Kam's body, then holding her after they finished.

"Us in our room," he answered.

She squeezed his hand and he squeezed back, wishing that the two of them in his room was really the only thing he was thinking about. Mother didn't belong in his head right now. It wasn't fair that she could kick in the door to his mind and make herself at home whenever the hell she wanted.

Lyle didn't want to continue with her pop psychology bullshit. He wanted to build something of his own. She had dragged him behind her on every speaking tour, for most of his life. He grew up as a tourist to every high-priced seminar. He became a citizen in his teens, when Mother gave him yet another role to play. This one meant priming her rooms for epiphanies, handing her son a scripted confession that acted like a key to unlock her transformative lessons.

Mother realized that middle-aged women responded especially well to an articulate teenaged boy who offered snippets of catchy wisdom while also seeming vulnerable. She coached him on a posture that made Lyle appear as though he was always seeking his mother's approval. The perfect bearing to sell bored, well-off housewives just about anything.

Lyle became the closer for the big-ticket offers, performing as proof that Mother's work had helped him to become the self-actualized young man he was. Audiences were always teary, and enamored with the idea that buying one of Ruthlessly Positive's Enlightenment Cruises or Cognitive Retreats would not only help them to become better people, but also make it easy to build a dream relationship with their children.

That led to her best-selling products so far. Mother shifted her focus to parent-child relationships when Lyle was twelve and she realized how well the moms in her seminars responded to his parroting of her admittedly catchy sayings.

Unfortunately, his growing into an adult had begun to threaten business as usual, so Mother kept trying to infantilize him, desperately aware that the parent-child angle wasn't sustainable, especially now that Lyle was looking more and more like a full-grown man.

He could finally see Mother for who she really was. A controlling show-biz mom who lived vicariously through her child, squeezing every cent out of his career and calling it her own.

I sacrificed everything to raise you! He could hear her in his head. *You owe me this.*

At his wit's end, Lyle had a near meltdown a few weeks ago. Mother had just barely managed to contain it during a seminar. She let him take some time for himself, to recharge and regroup while she figured out the next stage of their career.

But she couldn't have ever imagined that he would spend it like this.

"Do you see it?" Lyle tipped his chin toward the hotel.

"How could I not?"

The Hotel Bisou looked like a castle, rising from the street with smaller villas stacked into the lush hills behind it. This part of eScape was permanently dark, so a hundred thousand twinkle lights could tease the magic inside.

"Are you okay?" Kam asked. "You look … sad."

Lyle shrugged. "My friend keeps telling me to cheer up and that it could be worse; I could be stuck underground in a hole full of water. I know he means well."

It took a second for her to respond. Then: "You seriously have to stop it now."

"I—" Lyle stopped walking.

"What is it?" But then she saw it too.

It would have been shocking enough to see Mother walking toward them. That alone would've left him plenty to deal with. But Miley Riley was with her, and that was so much worse.

"Is that—"

"Yes," Lyle said.

Seconds later Miley and Mother were standing in front of them. He wanted to turn and look at Kam to make sure she was okay, but his gaze fixed on Mother, trying to read the runes in her eyes. What was she up to?

He never wanted to date Miley in the first place, and had only done so because Mother made him. A "win-win situation," she'd said. Miley needed a ratings boost, and their dating would funnel young women into the Ruthlessly Positive program that they wouldn't have access to otherwise.

No one had spoken, but the situation was still already out of control. Besides Mother and Miley, his ex-girlfriend's entourage was standing behind her, two boys, two girls, and two gender-fluid assholes Lyle had never been able to stand.

And sure as shit, that was the press clustered behind the lot of them, holding their cameras and mics, a woman in a trench coat and fedora pushing her way to the front. No surprise, since nothing attracted a crowd like a crowd; a mass of squealing guys and gals (mostly gals) were assembling in a horde, phones out to record whatever momentous, or disastrous, event might be about to unfold.

Lyle and Kam were apparently the only ones who didn't get the script.

He snatched his hand out of Kam's, surprising and disappointing himself as he did.

Kam gasped as he cringed.

Lyle could smell the confusion and surprise.

"Why are you dressed like that?" Mother asked him.

"And what are you doing with *that girl?*" Miley unwrapped a lollypop and tucked it into her mouth, very aware of the cameras all around her.

"What are *you* doing here?" Lyle didn't care who answered, he was only buying time.

"We're looking for you," Mother said.

"It's been a long time," Miley cooed, again for the cameras.

Kam was now at least three full steps behind him, and he could feel her wanting to run.

Miley closed the distance between them, leaving Mother behind as she came up to Lyle, wrapped her arms around his neck, then planted a wet kiss on his cheek while grinding against his leg."

"Stop that!" Lyle barked, pulling away.

The crowd laughed. They either thought he was kidding or were amused by what was probably a very red face. Emotions were much more visible inside eScape than they were outside of it.

Miley ignored him, still coming closer, still sliding her body against his. It was kind of gross when she did it a couple of years ago, but Lyle was a man now, and the last thing he needed was his own mother pimping him out.

I'm on a date!

It was only four words, and he needed to say them, but Lyle couldn't manage to get them out of his mouth. Mother and Miley had descended upon him in a suffocating rush.

He turned around to check on Kam, but Mother yanked on his arm, wrenching his gaze back toward them.

Kam was walking away, but he couldn't let that happen. He wanted to call out, beg her not to abandon him.

The thought filled him with a sudden and unreasonable anger. His rage was wrong, but Lyle felt it anyway. Kam was renouncing him, walking away from what they had, before either one of them even got the chance to have it.

His feelings weren't rational; what was she supposed to do? Unless Kam wanted to cause a scene, leaving was her only choice. How could he blame her for not wanting to go toe-to-toe with Miley and Mother and what felt like a thousand cameras capturing the moment for a million voyeurs to later enjoy?

His fans were hungry for news, and his vanishing act a few months ago had only multiplied the horde. He needed some alone time, so Lyle started going inside eScape under the name of Jaxon. Did a lot of Deep Spells whenever he could get away from Mother long enough to avoid her needling questions. The media was always talking about him, wondering about where he had gone and what he was up to, and doing it out loud. Good-natured yet incessant nagging for him to finally "return to work."

But Lyle had a hard time returning to a world that felt even more artificial than the petaflops of data management that made this place look so real.

Lyle glanced over his shoulder again, hoping to see

Kam standing behind him. She was gone, along with his courage, so he did the only thing he could do to get through the moment, considering the future he could have by playing his cards right.

Lyle turned to the throng of cameras and smiled.

Chapter Fourteen

Kam

KAM WASN'T EVER SUPPOSED to feel miserable at the Malt Shoppe.

That was the whole reason she had bought the place. An always-available booth that kept her cozy and served Kam like a second home inside eScape. A place to commiserate with friends, or be alone, depending on her mood.

But she couldn't just ignore what happened to her in front of the Hotel Bisou. Getting discarded like that, it was hard for Kam to think about anything else. She spent half her time wishing they had never left Lyle's special room inside eScape — he shouldn't have stopped her from undressing; she wanted it and so did he. The rest of her time, Kam wished she'd never met him.

It was true and it wasn't. Fire and ice. A migraine that made its home in her stomach.

When unlimited shakes at the Malt Shoppe could no longer cut it, Kam invited her friends over to improve her mood. But she was being stupid, and really should have known. Of course they would make everything worse.

"There's no way he really loves her," Kelso said.

Dee laughed. "Or so Raquel keeps insisting!"

"I'm glad he has someone to practice on. But if Lyle thinks that Miley Riley can do *anything* better than me, he's crazy."

Kelso turned to Raquel. "You mean anything better than you, besides singing, or dancing, or—"

"I meant in bed."

"You have an awfully high opinion yourself," Dee said. "I'm sure Miley Riley has been around. She could probably teach you a thing or two."

"She means in bed," Kelso clarified.

"Screw you both," Raquel said.

"No thanks." Dee made a face. "We're not available just because Lyle prefers Miley to you. Sorry."

"You should be sorry that you'll never know what he looks like naked."

Dee made another face. "*You'll* never get another chance. Did you see what Miley was wearing? I'm sure she can take care of Lyle just fine."

Kelso whistled. "Her pants were so tight I could see her religion."

Everyone laughed, except Kam.

"Need another milkshake?" Kelso asked.

She gave the table a half-smile. "I'm fine."

No one gave a shit anyway.

"If you really want to meet him in person, you should go on that couples' retreat," Dee suggested.

"Oh right," scoffed Raquel. "Because I'll really have a chance with Miley there. And besides, I'd need a fake boyfriend."

"Kelso will do it," Dee offered.

"She's right," Kelso said.

"What do you think it's like?" Raquel asked, seeming to take the suggestion seriously.

"Lush gardens full of tropical flowers, pool suites with full bars, sailing at sunset ..." Dee started.

"Amazing restaurants, a kick-ass night life, in-suite jacuzzis, golf courses—" Kelso tried to finish before Raquel cut him off.

"Like you're really going to play golf! And I meant the event itself, not the accommodations. If I want some resort time, I'll ask Daddy if I can go to the Montage or whatever. I'm asking what you think the couples' retreat is like."

"You heard the announcement, same as we did," Dee admonished Raquel, before reciting Lyle's pitch in an almost professorial tone. "The Two as One Retreat is your exclusive chance to look inward and focus on yourself so you can each give more to one another for the rest of your life. This elite event will have discussions, lectures, and role-play to rebuild your relationship. Combined with a romantic vacation, this exclusive couples getaway will pave the path to a deeper relationship that will boost intimacy and make you both glow with happiness."

"You sound like a commercial," Raquel said. "And that still doesn't tell me what you think the retreat will be like."

"Why don't you ask Kam?" Kelso looked at her stirring her milkshake with a long metal spoon. "She hasn't said anything since last week."

Kam replied in a monotone. "There were three uses of the word *exclusive* in Dee's pitch. If that was truly word-for-word, then Lyle Grace must really need us all to know how high class he really is."

"Ooh ..." Dee cooed. "Sounds like someone is *jealous*."

"I'm not jealous," Kam said, slipping the now vanilla-flavored spoon into her mouth.

But she did feel the envy. And worse, Kam was depressed. That Lyle didn't stand up to his mom for her, doing what he'd always done instead, letting her use him as a puppet while his pop star ex-girlfriend crawled all over him like a tree she was trying to climb.

The whole thing made her furious, because now Kam couldn't help but see Lyle as either a liar or a coward, and she didn't know which was worse.

What happened to all of those things he'd told her in private? A litany of confessions Kam had taken to heart. Now she felt used. Not just because she was willing to fully give herself to him. She wasn't one of those girls who thought that sex inside eScape "didn't really count." Of course it did. Even if their bodies weren't pressed together in real life, emotions and bodily responses were exactly the same.

They both wanted it, and Kam would have been fine with whatever happened. Her real problem was that Lyle bled all of his feelings out in front of her. He was two-faced, telling her one thing behind a closed door while pretending that everything was shiny and happy on the other side of it.

The hypocrisy made her want to cry.

But for now, like she'd been doing for more than a day, Kam had to keep ignoring it.

"I think she's jealous," Kelso said, since there had been several seconds without anyone talking.

"And what exactly is it that I'm jealous about?" Kam asked, pushing the milkshake away from her.

"You act like you're not totally in love with him when we all know you are." Raquel looked at Kam, daring her friend to reply. "You always get that look on your face whenever his name comes up."

"Maybe that's because I think he's stupid," Kam said.

The rest of them traded a look.

But Raquel said, "Or because you're totally in love with him."

"Yeah," Kelso laughed, "or you're totally in love with him."

That was it. Kam had finally boiled over. Her blood was lava and her cells like liquid fire. Slamming her palms onto the table she yelled, "You're all so stupid — don't any of you realize that Ruthless Positivity is all a crock of shit?"

Onlookers were eyeing their table now. For the first time, her friends might start taking her seriously. None of them understood the depth of her anger. Raquel was looking at Kam like she might be nuts, but Kelso and Dee were laughing.

"Since when?" Kelso asked.

"Since the first time Julia Grace ever said anything about it."

Clearly those were fighting words, the way the table had turned on her.

They all looked rabid, Raquel most of all.

But Dee spoke first, and did so with a snarl. "You have no idea what you're talking about."

Kelso and Raquel were staring at Kam, waiting for her to respond.

She made them wait, elongating the moment as she carefully selected her words, trying to decide as she did whether it was better to have them all out of her life just for right now, or — more likely — forever. She took a long sip of her milkshake, then finally said what was on her mind.

"Julia Grace isn't an infallible, all-knowing oracle, you know. She's a businessperson with a booming business and products to sell. Products that you all buy, because you're too dim to see all the smoke and mirrors. Most gurus are barely qualified to give life advice, and Julia Grace is among the worst of them!"

Several of the Malt Shoppe's booths were turned toward her table, with too many customers now staring. She owned this place — wasn't there anything she could do about that?

Dee's face was the color of a cranberry. "You have no right to disrespect Lyle Grace like that."

"I'm not—"

"We always knew there was something wrong with you," Kelso cut her off.

Raquel turned to both him and Dee, showing Kam only her shoulder. "It's like she was born poor or something."

The three of them laughed.

Kam looked down at the shake, imagining herself hurling whatever was left in there all over Raquel. She wanted to pull Dee's hair and scratch Kelso's face. Scream until her throat was bloody.

But she couldn't do any of that, so she took a deep breath, then leaned forward and growled, "Get out."

"You can't tell us where to go," Dee said.

"Get. Out," Kam repeated.

Her former friends started laughing even louder.

"GET OUT!" she yelled.

Then they were suddenly gone from the table and Kam was looking across the Malt Shoppe, staring at the three of them standing on the other side of a long oval wall-sized window, each one staring back, just as perplexed as the others.

Roughly a third of the Shoppe was looking at Kam, another third had their gazes turned outside to her former friends, while the remaining diners bounced between the two sights like balls in a volley over the net.

"You're banned from the Malt Shoppe!"

Some of the spectators looking at her swiveled their heads toward the group, eager to see its reaction. Raquel's rage was the loudest. She stepped in front of Kelso and Dee, violently opened the door, and marched back into the Malt Shoppe.

But one step into the place and Raquel materialized outside, shunted back behind her friends.

Kam wanted to frame their baffled expressions and hang them on her grimy, crumbling walls at home. Or maybe here, on the perfectly nostalgic walls of the Malt Shoppe.

Dee and Kelso tried next, marching together. Same result, a split-second later they were both staring at the back of Raquel's well-coiffed mane.

"How are you doing that?" Kelso yelled at her.

"I own this place, and your permissions have been revoked!"

Raquel was already looking back at Kam through the window, now Kelso and Dee had joined her.

"You'll be sorry for this!" Raquel cried out.

"I'm already sorry I met you!"

Mobiles were out, joining the handful that were already capturing her outburst for any citizens of eScape unlucky enough to have missed the live show. Kam's former friends surrendered, leaving the Shoppe in a huff. But there was nothing she could do to avoid the unwanted attention coming her way now.

Kam cringed, picturing Lyle's face when he saw her tantrum later. Of course it would go viral. Maybe he wouldn't care, holed up in the Hotel Bisou with Miley Riley, doing whatever his mother ordered him to do. She could only imagine, and the images made her sick.

But perhaps this was for the best. A good thing, her

finally having the courage to say what she really thought, and doing it in public. Kam might even feel great about that, if she allowed herself to. Condemning her ridiculously entitled friends didn't hurt, not like she thought it would.

No matter what happened between her and Lyle, at least he had given her that. Kam already knew how great it felt to say the truth out loud to herself, but now she knew how great it could also feel to say it loud in a room full of strangers.

And for that, she was grateful.

Kam wished she didn't care, but she couldn't help herself.

So she closed her eyes and wondered what Lyle was thinking.

Chapter Fifteen

Lyle

LYLE WOKE up in the real world, furious at Mother.

He'd smiled for the cameras and muscled through the moment, but he wasn't about to let her win. She beat him home, out of her Nest and standing with her arms crossed, glaring down at Lyle while waiting for him to emerge. Her every move was calculated. She stood over Lyle and Miley long enough to make sure he didn't step out of bounds in front of all those cameras, but vanished from eScape far enough ahead of Lyle to leave her with a proper advantage.

It was wrong, the way she lorded over him. Nest time was private and Lyle couldn't have been any more vulnerable. Mother might as well have been watching him masturbate.

No one spoke; Lyle seethed as she continued to stare at him, unwilling to break their stalemate.

The nausea passed and he finally stepped all the way from the Nest. He looked around, still not saying a word to

Mother, but relieved to see that the other two pods were empty. Meaning, Miley had logged in from her own Nest, in her own apartment, or lair, or wherever succubi and harpies lay dormant for the night. Getting ambushed in eScape and then having to deal with Mother outside of it was more than enough — Lyle was glad he wouldn't have to deal with that trampy little tart until later, if at all.

Maybe he could get away without ever seeing Miley Riley again, but only if he realized that every move mattered. Mother was the ultimate strategist, and for the first time in Lyle's life he would have to outplay her.

"How did you know where to find me?" He cracked the quiet, giving her an easy win up front to hopefully disarm her for later.

"Ha," she scoffed. "You think I don't know what you're up to?"

Lyle shrugged. "I guess I believed it when you promised me time to figure things out, and the space to make it happen."

"I did give you space."

"While monitoring me."

"I wasn't monitoring you, Lyle. Who was that little twit you were with?"

"How did you know where to find me?" Lyle asked again.

"*Who was that little twit you were with?*"

"I asked you first."

"This isn't kindergarten."

"Then stop treating me like a kindergartner. You want to know who I was with, then you need to tell me why you ambushed us in front of the hotel. And with *Miley fucking Riley.*"

"Don't you swear at me."

Fuck you, Mother. "Then for the third time: how did you know where to find me?"

"Do you think you're hard to find?" She laughed. "Don't you realize that I have eyes and ears everywhere, because people in this world are loyal to me. And whether you're in the real world or eScape, you'll never be anything more than my son."

Lyle let it go, bigger wins would be coming. "You still haven't answered the question."

"It's not a big mystery, Lyle. I got an alert the second you logged into the Hotel Bisou. There's only one reason you would be going there. You were about to make a terrible branding mistake, and that could hurt us both. I obviously had to stop it."

"You're delusional." Lyle had spoken those words in eScape before, but saying them out loud in the real world was like a hot shot of whiskey. "I was going to the hotel in private. No one would have known if you hadn't shown up."

"People would have found out."

"So what if they did? I'm almost twenty-one years old — are you seriously saying that I'm not old enough to have a relationship of my own? That you needed to ambush me because—"

"I didn't *ambush* you, Lyle. You're being ridiculous right now. I was acting in your best interests. You're clearly on the verge of another meltdown if you think you're going to get away with—"

"*Another* meltdown?"

"—this bullshit of starting your own business."

"So *that's* what this is about?" Of course it was.

"I've given you everything, and now you're trying to ruin it all."

"I'm not ruining anything, Mother. I'm building something for myself."

"By using my toolbox and all of my tools."

Lyle chuckled to himself.

"How dare you laugh at me."

"How dare you drag Miley back into my life." He kept his voice even, but Lyle was boiling under his skin. They were already bobbing in uncharted waters and he had no idea where this argument might be going.

"Miley has always been good for your image."

"*Good for my image?*" Lyle stared at Mother.

"Yes, Lyle. Good for your image. At least one of us needs to care about that."

"If there's one area of my life where image shouldn't matter at all, it's my dating life!"

"Lower your voice, you're losing control."

"I'm not doing this anymore, Mother. You're too controlling, and I need something of my own."

"I'm not *too controlling*, Lyle. I'm the only one looking out for you like—"

"BULLSHIT!"

The force of his bellow forced Mother to fall back a step. Her eyes widened and her bottom lip began to tremble. She didn't issue yet another warning not to swear or yell at her. Lyle didn't like that he had to yell for her to listen, nor could he deny the obvious truth.

Softer he said, "You are too controlling, and you don't know how to listen to me. You put unrealistic demands on my time and attention, always expecting me to drop everything the second you need me. And worse, you make me feel like I'm responsible for your emotional well-being."

"That's ridiculous. I am perfectly capable of taking care of my emotional self — let's not forget that I'm the author of *Ruthlessly Positive*."

Lyle rolled his eyes. "Like anyone could ever forget it."

"You can't just—"

"*You make me sad when you go a day without talking to me.* That's a bullshit thing to say to your kid, whether you realize it or not. It makes me responsible for your emotions, and feel like I have to lie—"

"You don't *have* to lie."

"To avoid disappointing you. That was bad enough when I was a kid, but I'm not a kid anymore, and I should be able to spend my own time however I want to. I'm an adult, I'm responsible for my own decisions, I'm the one who has to—"

"Then you should be making better ones."

"—deal with the consequences of my actions. So I should get to make my own choices."

"You *do* make your own choices, Lyle."

"No." He shook his head. "I don't. I'm expected to check in with you before every major decision and—"

"That's because your business is my business and—"

"I don't want to be in business with you anymore!"

She laughed. "You really expect that you'll have anything without me?"

"That. Right there!" Lyle jabbed his finger at her. "That's exactly what I'm talking about. If we had a healthy relationship, you would be proud instead of being jealous of me. You'd celebrate my best qualities and help—"

"*Celebrate your best qualities?* You ungrateful little shit — I've built an entire business around you."

He shook his head again. "That was always for you, never for me."

"Everything I've ever done is for you."

"Including pimping me out to Miley Riley."

"Ha," she scoffed. "I'm hardly 'pimping you out.'"

"Okay, Mother."

"Don't *okay* me, Lyle. I've allowed you to have your little tantrum, but let's be done with that. Right now you need to—"

"Step in line? Do exactly as you say, or suffer the consequences — is that right?"

"This is really very simple, Lyle," she calmly responded. "I own the business, so you can either continue to be a part of what I've built and do as I say, or I can cut you out and you'll get nothing."

"That's wrong and you know it."

"What you're doing is *wrong*, challenging me like this when I've given you the life of a prince."

"I'm a prisoner and both of us know it."

She scoffed again. "So much drama. I didn't know you could act like this; maybe you should be doing more for us on stage."

"So that's it?" His heart was pounding. Lyle had been imagining this exact moment for a while now. Sometimes it came in a dream and others in a nightmare, but deep in his heart he'd always known exactly how this would end. "That's the ultimatum? I either do what you say or you cut me out of the trust?"

"Your words, not mine." Mother stared at him, her face hard, daring him to challenge her again. "Should I have Doctor Bryant prescribe you something for your anxiety?"

"I'm not anxious! I'm pissed. I don't need my doctor." Lyle had spent years of his youth on various sedatives or mood stabilizers whenever he "acted up."

But he didn't have ADHD or any other mental issues that required medication.

"You're right. You don't need meds. You merely require a mental adjustment. Some Ruthless Positivity."

Despite his suspicions that this was exactly how things

would ultimately go, it was still the first time Lyle was forced to both admit and accept his reality. He had to make a decision, even if it was one he could never come back from.

"Fine. I accept your terms. Fuck my trust. I'll go my own way and do my own thing. We'll see who follows me, and who stays with—"

She laughed, long and hard. It was a put-on, and Lyle knew what she was doing, but still her derision was a cold blade between his warm ribs. She wasn't just unfazed. Somehow, despite Lyle's threat, Mother still seemed so thoroughly in control.

She sighed, long and dramatic. "This was always my biggest worry, and now here it is."

"What? That I'd start my own thing?" Lyle asked, falling right into her trap.

"No. I don't like that now I'll have to watch you fail, but I worried that you'd turn into your father one day. Now here we are."

Lyle looked at her. He had no idea what to do with that.

She shook her head in pity. "There are consequences for that kind of behavior, and I'm sorry, Lyle, but I simply cannot save you from them. I suggest that you think long and hard about what kind of life you want."

"I know exactly what kind of life I want."

"Do you?" Mother raised her eyebrows. "Because I think what we have here is a serious loss of perspective on your part. I don't think you really understand what the world is like, or how much I've given to you. Your life has been filled with every material comfort. You've experienced fame and respect that you never had to work for. You've mingled with the richest—"

"I don't care about any of that!"

"Of course you do. And you'll find out exactly how much you care when you're living like your derelict, good-for-nothing father."

In the past, being shamed with Baker's bad behavior always made him back down. But things had changed, and Lyle was better than that now. He could clearly hear the threat behind her words. Mother would give her son the same drugs she gave to her husband, to make him easier to control.

There was only one way out of this.

He ignored the acidic stew in his stomach, pretended his throat wasn't burning, then gave Mother the long sigh full of surrender she was waiting for.

"I'll do whatever you want me to. But no more Miley, under any circumstances."

"Fine," Mother said. "But let's say no girls at all. I don't want you anywhere near that trollop."

Lyle agreed out loud, just not in his head.

Kam wasn't a trollop, she was the woman who might just save his life.

So the second Mother was out of the room he sent her a message:

I need to see you immediately.

Chapter Sixteen

Kam

KAM CHECKED HER PHONE, and sure enough she saw another message from Lyle.

She ignored that one, too.

He acted like Kam should be living at his beck and call. *I need to see you immediately; Please, can we talk; I'm sorry about what happened … can you please respond to me?; I really need to talk to you.*

Kam didn't care about what *he* needed. Or that he was supposedly sorry.

Lyle hadn't done the right thing when he had the chance and that was all that mattered. He hurt her. Worse than the disease that had been chewing through her body for years. Worse than the excruciating, almost unendurable process that was slowly preparing Kam for an eternity in eScape. Worse than her father, because she had stopped believing in him long before he went nuts enough to step in front of a bus.

She could still feel Lyle snatching his hand away from

153

hers. Still see him cringing as she gasped. Still hear him asking his mother why she and that skank were there, though he never used that word. But Kam couldn't hear Lyle defending her, because that never even came close to happening.

Miley Riley. Of all the obnoxious pop stars in the world, she was the most ridiculous. And the most vacuous. Not exactly one of the most famous, but notable enough. Everything about her turned Kam's stomach. The nose ring; the barbed wire bracelet tattooed on her wrist; pink hair in Princess Leah buns; the occasional cat ears; shoes that cost more than a car; and a wardrobe that left little to the imagination.

Kam wasn't judgmental; if any of Miley Riley's getup was authentic, then Kam wouldn't have cared at all. Nor did she care if a woman showed some skin. But Miley was clearly a product from head to toe, and one Kam couldn't imagine anyone ever wanting to buy. Even her name was worse than absurd, something she'd expect to see in a skit about preposterous pop stars and the plebes who adored them.

No, Kam wouldn't be calling him back. Not now or any time soon.

She'd been alone before. Had lived her entire life that way. But it was never worse than this, because now Kam knew what she'd been missing. Her friends were mostly empty, but at least they occasionally listened to her, and didn't mind her being around. When you had zero friends, almost any would do, and they were her first.

Then Lyle … Kam had never expected that. Wouldn't have dared to. She didn't ask for Lyle Grace to fall into her life like that. Or maybe on top of it. She should never have trusted him, or let herself go so carelessly. Now she had to deal with the consequences of her misplaced faith. Lyle made her feel disposable, and that was even worse than the abandonment. Kam could spend the rest of her life crying, and not just from the agony Pibly was inflicting upon her, but from the bewildering ache that came out of nowhere to stain her present and poison her future.

Picture a very still lake with—

"Don't tell me what to think," Kam told the AI again.

Your stress levels are rising. I'm only—

"I know what you're trying to do. But you can't just tell me to picture a lake or a meadow or my special cave and expect that I'll calm down a second later. It doesn't work like that."

Countless studies, lab tests, and field results have more than proven—

"You're an AI. Are you really telling me that they're 'countless?'"

It's a common expression. Using them makes it easier to relate—

"Well, you're doing a terrible job."

I am sorry for the pain you're going through.

"No you're not. You're an AI, but thanks."

It didn't respond, and Kam was grateful. The procedure was painful enough without Pibly piping platitudes into her earpiece and giving her unnecessary mental direction. She chose to put herself through this; she could deal with the agony in her own way.

Part medical, part pure tech, Kam was preparing herself for a permanent upload to eScape. This was where being a sorceress at coding paid off. Not only did she have the know-how to pull off the impossible, she had developed the network to assemble every one of the illegal components required to turn the theoretical into a final result, and now that reality was but a matter of time.

One day, she was sure, the afterlife would be available to everyone. But right now there weren't more than a hundred people in the world who could do what Kam was preparing to do.

You're spending too much time in Deep Spell, Pibly started in on her again.

"So you keep telling me."

Pibly had a point. Kam was weak and kept fumbling with the equipment, which kept nicking her slow-to-heal body. The AI was guiding her through the process, but it couldn't exactly move Kam's fingers for her.

You need to be more conservative with both your on and offline energy. Focus on short bursts for now, until you're ready to upload for good.

"When was the last time you saw me in a Deep Spell?"

You logged out of eScape early during your last two sessions, but only because duress within the simulation triggered your flight response. Neither time was a premeditated action on your part. I predict with a rather high probability that your next trip will be a Deep Spell as—

"You're like a Magic 8-Ball with a worse personality."

Magic 8-Balls don't have personalities.

"Maybe you just haven't met the right one."

If your body degrades too far, it could interfere with the upload.

Kam swallowed. That was the only one of the AI's stupid arguments that it made any sense to worry about. Obviously, the upload couldn't fail. Because then she would be dead without her bonus round, and the last few years of her life would have been a total waste. She would have squandered them on preparing for her ultimate failure instead of living in full with the little she had.

And the increasingly rapid deterioration was all her fault.

Kam's body degraded just fine on its own, but intense emotions accelerated the deterioration. Good and bad, both were doing her in. Seeing Lyle sent a surge of adrenaline and other hormones through her body. The cocktail spiked whenever she felt yet another flutter of affection or warmth, rejection or ire, giddy hope or abject despair.

It's like her body was trying to catch up after all the years spent repressing her emotions. A lifetime of throttling her thoughts for fear of punishment. Physical and emotional, her father enjoyed them both. He never quite smiled while doling out the worst of it, but Kam could feel his pleasure. Almost a relief, as though something inside him had finally been vented. Like the bodily gratification of an ass hitting the toilet seat just in time.

Kam was young when she first made the box. Small as possible, she kept it inside her and crammed every trouble-some emotion within it. But now they had snaked their way out, and she had no way of ever getting them back into the box.

Perhaps it's time for a pill, Pibly suggested.

That might be some advice worth taking. Her supply was dwindling, but doing so could help compensate for some of the more severe damage that had already been done.

"I'm guessing you wouldn't suggest it if taking a pill was a bad idea."

That is correct.

"How many do I have left?"

Fourteen.

The final upload would take her days, and she'd have to be constantly medicated during that time. Pibly esti-mated needing nine to twelve pills to keep Kam stable throughout the process. But she should also have an extra one or two for emergencies, in case the upload ran long. Going without a pill at any point during the process was non-negotiable. She needed the chemicals to buffer the damage uploading would do to her brain, and ensure she didn't end up with a lobotomized avatar.

The pills weren't easy to get. Underground, ridiculously expensive, and a constantly moving target. Kam had access to unlimited funds, but she had to hack in the right places and keep herself invisible. That took time she didn't have.

"One pill," she finally agreed, fumbling for the small bottle sitting on the rolling cart beside her.

I also suggest that you refill your Dising prescription.

"No thanks."

It's my job to—

"I'm super clear on your job, but that stuff makes me way too foggy."

Dising regulates your hormones. You shouldn't go back into eScape without a dose. It will keep your emotions on an even keel until you are ready to up—

"No worries there, Pibly. I have no intention of going inside eScape."

You've practically been living inside the—

"Right. And look at all it's done for me."

Pibly didn't respond, but Kam had more to say and no one else around.

"Now that I've seen Lyle's true colors, I don't want to be anywhere near the place. I won't spend another second logged in until I'm ready to log in for good. He can go to hell in the meantime."

She heard a slight hum in her earpiece and imagined Pibly thinking, maybe even wanting to ask Kam a question. She went ahead and answered the query.

"I've spent the last several years of my life setting all of this up." Her voice rose in both volume and pitch. "I'm not about to blow it for some two-faced self-help guru with *serious* mommy issues."

Pibly still didn't respond, but that was fine. Kam was done talking to her stupid AI.

But thinking about it, maybe she would have to go inside at least one more time. To test her new avatar, which she absolutely would have to design. She would need to swap her old one out, because it was ruined. More specifically, Lyle had destroyed it. She couldn't trust that he wouldn't report her and get her locked out of the system just to save himself.

She knew his secret. And if the eScape police discovered the backdoor she'd created for herself, they would design security protocols that would make it impossible for her to build another one.

Would you like to talk about it? Pibly asked.

"Talk about what?" But she knew.

Your encounters with Lyle Grace. They, more than anything else, seemed to have upset you. A conversation could—

"How about you shove it instead?"

I do suggest you unburden yourself.

"Maybe I should lighten the load by ditching my annoying AI. Its name is Pibly and it really sucks."

Pibly didn't respond.

Sure, it would probably feel great to unburden herself by talking about Lyle, even it was only venting to an AI. But she didn't need to talk about him, or even want to think about him. The pain was excruciating enough, burning her insides to ash by the feel of it.

She would never see Lyle Grace again, and Kam was fine with that.

But Kam was also wrong.

Chapter Seventeen

Lyle

LYLE SCURRIED DOWN THE STREET, feeling frantic, surprised by the real-world emotion intruding on him here on this digital boulevard. eScape was supposed to be an *escape*, the place to forget about all of the bullshit in his life, same as everyone else.

But the real world had failed him, and now this one was doing the same damn thing.

Mother was a monster. Lyle had to placate her, even if he couldn't stand to be near her. That strategy was fine, but only if he could get the other side to play out. And for that, he needed Kam. He needed her to hear him, to understand that he never ever wanted to hurt her, and that he felt worse about what he'd done than he'd ever felt about anything else in his entire life.

Lyle walked even faster, quickly closing the distance between himself and the Malt Shoppe.

He didn't know where else to look, or how else he might be able to get a hold of her. Kam hadn't answered any of his increasingly desperate messages. eScape was infinite for anyone who didn't want to be found, but the Malt Shoppe seemed to be more than a hot spot for Kam — the way she talked about it, the place was more like a second home.

But something stirred in his stomach when Lyle was still just far off enough to not quite understand what he was seeing, then the feeling worsened by the step. Until he was frozen, standing in front of the boarded Malt Shoppe, squinting at a sign he wished was in a different language so he wouldn't have to process the truth, though just looking at the place made the message apparent enough.

The Malt Shoppe is closed for renovations until further notice.

Except that didn't make sense. Nothing ever needed to close "for renovations." Reconditioning or redecorations were done in a blink once their owner covered the cost.

He pounded on the front door and both of the large picture windows to either side. For several minutes, not that he expected anyone to answer. He surveyed the neighbors. But no one inside Full Moon Pizza, Aladdin's Palace, or Angel's Barbecue had any idea why the Shoppe was closed, how long it might be shuttered, or if there was any way to get in touch with the owner. Worse, it didn't seem like any of the people Lyle asked could have possibly cared less.

He looked down the long row of digital distractions, knowing he had to surrender. eScape was too big for someone who wanted to disappear, and Lyle …

… had an idea.

"Hey Vox …"

Let me guess, you would like help locating Miss Kam in the real world.

"Yes. Is that possible?"

Without her name it will be.

Lyle sighed. "That's what I—"

Or at least it would be, if I didn't already have her assistant in my network.

"You can do that? Talk to Pibly directly?"

I'm doing it now.

"Oh," Lyle said, surprised. "What's it saying?"

Lyle repeated his question twice before falling silent, waiting for Vox to finish talking to Kam's AI. The timing felt weird. Conversation was a human thing; if Vox and Pibly were both ones and zeroes, then shouldn't any dialogue between them last only seconds at most?

We have a location, Vox finally announced.

"In eScape, or—"

In the real world, but I promised that I would talk to you before your exit.

"Talk to me about what?" Lyle didn't like the sound of that, and still felt weirded out by the two AIs having a conversation, especially one that lasted longer than a few seconds.

Pibly has violated its user's privacy by informing us of her location. As a fellow assistant I can assure you this was not easy to do.

"But we have a physical address?"

Yes, but I was only able to persuade Pibly because I explained how sorry you were, and how much you wanted or perhaps even needed to apologize. As an AI extension of Kam, Pibly could feel how much she needed for that to happen.

"So, she's sad right now?" Lyle asked, feeling happier than he wanted to admit.

It's more than her being sad. Pibly is concerned that Kam's emotional turmoil will prevent her from uploading.

"Prevent her from uploading? Why the hell would that matter? Isn't that what eScape is for, so people have a place they can go when they're sad?"

Kam is seeking a more … permanent solution.

Vox was even pausing his delivery like a human, and that was really starting to piss Lyle off.

"What's that supposed to mean? What sort of a permanent solution?"

Kam is looking to upload herself permanently into eScape, so she can live inside it forever.

"You can't do that!"

Lyle didn't actually know if you could or couldn't, though it sure didn't sound right. He would have heard, if for no other reason than it would have altered Mother's retirement plans significantly.

It is possible, but not easy, and highly dangerous. Pibly is worried that Kam's body has degraded too much for a final upload. She is already weak and the intensity of her emotions are making it impossible for her to heal.

"I'll make everything better," Lyle promised.

That's what we need to discuss …

"What are you trying to say?"

You are expecting that your presence will remedy the situation. You picture Kam running into your arms, and imagine that things will be back to the way they were simply because you want them to be. But Pibly says that she's hurt, and the best thing for you is to apologize, then leave her alone.

"Leave her alone?"

You have impaired her emotional balance, so yes, it's necessary to repair it before she can move on. But this isn't like sewing a hole in a sock, Lyle. You're—

"I get it, you don't have to keep talking." The words were like balls of snot in his throat. A hard swallow before he could finish, then, "I promise that I'll do everything in my power to help Kam recover her emotional balance, even if that means promising to leave her alone forever. Now, can we please get out of here?"

Very well.

Vox started the process of pulling Lyle out of his Deep Spell while working to keep himself from getting sick. If he started throwing up in eScape, his throat would be burning when he opened his blurry eyes back in the real world.

"Will she be okay?" Lyle asked as he began to fade, away from the artifice and into reality.

Her body is weak. She is dying.

"Is it possible that she'll actually die?" He couldn't stand to consider the possibility.

Of course. That is the definition of dying.

He throttled his emotions, wanting to cry, but holding the tears until he was safely on the other side. Feelings were magnified when going either in or out of eScape. If you went in happy, your avatar stayed over the moon. Leave with so much as a hint of sorrow, and a person's very real body might be blinking its eyes in despair.

Calm your mind or I can't get you to her.

"I know," Lyle said.

Vox didn't argue. The AI knew he was doing his best.

He regulated his breathing, in and out as he emptied his thoughts. Lyle was shaken by the thought that Kam might literally die. He suspected things were bad, and that she'd been keeping the worst of it from him even before Pibly spilled more of the beans, but he still never thought she was in danger of leaving this world. Of leaving him, and abandoning any chance he had of a happy life away from the one he'd been drifting through on autopilot and under his mother's thumb.

"I'll do whatever I can," Lyle promised Vox, though he was speaking mostly to himself, calming his body and mind enough to leave his Deep Spell without emotional trauma. "Whatever it takes to heal Kam, and keep her out of danger."

He never finished the thought. Yes, of course Lyle

would do whatever it took to get her safely uploaded into eScape. Once she was safe inside, he'd have the rest of his life to make things right.

Lyle opened his eyes, disoriented and blinking, but still glad to be back in the real world.

Vox was in his ears, but everything was wrapped in gauze and Lyle couldn't hear much more than a staticky warble. He stepped out of the Nest, too fast and dizzy enough to fall on his face.

You need to wait a moment, Lyle. You know better than this.

He ignored Vox, leaving his room, then stepping into the elevator while still woozy, taking it to the parking garage where his vintage Valkyrie was waiting.

Lyle climbed inside the car. He didn't need to tell Vox where to go, the AI knew better than he did. The Aston Martin hummed as it started, then slightly louder as it soared out of the garage and onto the street, racing through Elysium toward the other side of town, still sucking air through his teeth in the luxurious cabin while working to reorient himself with reality.

Vox caught him up on the way, telling Lyle all that Pibly had told him. A horror show if true, Kam's upload would take her days, but her body wasn't stable enough to make it through the process. She was taking Dising to regulate her emotions, but she didn't have nearly enough, especially when accounting for the emergencies Pibly seemed so certain of.

The leather seats were soft against his back, but as neighborhoods decayed on the other side of his window Lyle began to feel worse and worse about the car he got for his eighteenth birthday. Really, the Valkyrie was just another way for Mother to keep him under her thumb. It had to cost significantly more than the ramshackle shanties he'd been passing for a while now.

And still the neighborhoods kept getting worse.

"This can't be right," Lyle muttered to himself.

There is no mistake in the address, Vox said as he kept the Valkyrie flying down the street.

He'd never been so far from his comfort zone. Affluent neighborhoods were now miles behind him. So were the dangerous areas and the boulevards lined with bags of garbage and homeless men and women using them for pillows.

Still the scenery continued to decay as his gleaming car drove deeper into the filthiest slums Lyle had ever seen or dared to imagine.

"THIS IS WHERE KAM LIVES?" Lyle shouted in horror to himself.

It is, Vox responded with an unnecessary confirmation.

He replayed an old conversation in his head, horrifying himself as he remembered standing next to Kam at that party full of the obnoxiously rich, now seeing their condescending bullshit through her eyes and wishing he'd done more to stick up for her.

He'd let it all pass — it wasn't his problem, after all. But now every remembered phrase entered his head with like the tip of a knife through his skin.

Lottery loser's more like it.

Lottery winners are the worst. They shouldn't even be here. They stink up the nicest neighborhoods inside eScape with their new money bullshit.

I heard he eats ground beef.

No, Jaxon, I don't think that lottery winners should be sharing the same neighborhoods with families who earned their fortunes a long time ago.

They can enjoy whatever they want inside eScape, I don't give a shit, but they should stick to the parts of this place that are open to everyone.

They can blow their credits on all the experiences they want, but they shouldn't have exclusive access because they haven't earned their place.

My mom says that most of us wouldn't have bought into this neighborhood if we'd known they'd open Elysium to just anyone.

They just need to be taught how to behave in a civilized way.

Lyle remembered the glitch in Kam's avatar and wondered if it had been a sign of her physical deterioration. One he had been too stupid, or at least too self-absorbed, to see.

"Is this as fast as we can go?"

Safely, yes.

But Lyle was sure he felt the Valkyrie go ever so slightly faster. He tried to stop the thought that kept cycling through his mind like a hiccup from hell:

What if she dies before I can find her?

Chapter Eighteen

Kam

Lyle Grace was the last thing Kam expected to see.

Pibly had warned her that he was coming, but she didn't believe it. Couldn't, really. Even though AI was incapable of lying. She somehow thought her assistant had managed to override the directive in an attempt to trigger her defense mechanisms, or affect her emotions in some way.

But now she would have to deal with it, because here he was, staring at Kam as she sat in a dilapidated shack made of garbage aluminum, and other refuse discarded by a population who had so much more than she ever could in this world.

Not that it mattered, she was on her way to having more than them for infinity. She'd be there soon. Once Kam was finished dealing with Lyle. After she started breathing again, when the horror and humiliation and dishonor of it all had dissipated like mist in the wind.

Kam thought the worst had already happened to her.

But no, it wasn't even close. This was beyond mortifying. Kam was thoroughly crushed. Not only had he seen the worst of her situation, Lyle now knew the truth. She'd gained access to eScape through illegitimate means.

In other words, Kam had stolen it.

She tried to talk, but couldn't.

Lyle's eyes were full of questions, but his lips were pursed in what was surely disgust.

Kam wanted to yell at Pibly, but she couldn't. All this modern technology, entire digital universes recreated in an effort to replace the anguish of everyday life, and still she had to speak out loud to her assistant. Goddamned AI should be able to read her thoughts.

But still looking at Lyle, still trading stares under a blanket of silence, still terrified to shatter the stillness for fear of what might follow, Kam redirected her rage where it belonged. At Lyle Grace, the little prince who dared to enter her hovel and invade her life without permission.

As though her poverty and illness had anything to do with him.

As though he had any right to be here, or anywhere near her.

As though he wasn't a trespasser on her property, and in her life.

Not that the cops would ever come. Kam could call them right now and they might make a drive-by tomorrow. If this were in Elysium they'd be here already. Pibly would have sent them a signal the second she knew something was wrong, and the authorities would have come running to protect her. Instead, Pibly had invited the intruder inside, and there wasn't a soul in the world to care what he did to Kam now that he was there.

Lyle finally blinked and looked away from her. He fixed his gaze and her heart started pounding, with indignity and disgrace — all the usual shit. But he wasn't looking around at the squalor like Kam expected. He was inspecting her Nest instead.

His pursed lips finally split into something a lot like a smile, then he stepped toward her, his hands looking extra large and his arms seeming so awfully long the way they dangled uncertainly at his side.

He was mocking her, judging her Nest made of refuse. It wasn't pretty, but Kam had turned debris and detritus into a working apparatus. So fuck him for judging her.

"You built your own Nest?" Lyle asked.

"Get a good look at the freak show, then get the hell out of here." Kam spoke slowly yet defiantly, careful not to snarl. "Slumming hours are over."

He blinked, surprised. "I don't think of you as a freak."

"I've seen your life," she scoffed.

"That's not fair, Kam. I'm—"

"You should go. Get back to Mother. Spend the rest of your life being a good little boy."

"I'm not—"

"Miley Riley is waiting for you, Lyle. Make sure—"

"You're being ugly, Kam." He paused, as though startled by his own words. "I don't care about any of this." He gestured around, maybe at her Nest, though it could have been her entire rotting flat. "But I do care about you being unfair."

For the first time Kam noticed a new ache carved onto his face. This wasn't an avatar, it was real life, and this man couldn't hide the pain in darkened eyes or sagging cheeks.

Kam wanted to say sorry, but she couldn't.

You should apologize, Pibly suggested.

She wanted to tell her AI to fuck off, but Kam couldn't say that either.

171

"I didn't choose the life I have," Lyle continued. "I was born into it, same as you."

"Well, you sure weren't willing to risk it!"

"Of course I'm willing to risk it. That's why I'm here."

"You weren't willing to risk it by making your own decisions! Your mother decides *everything* for you, Lyle — INCLUDING WHO SHE EXPECTS YOU TO FUCK!"

Kam's rage was surprising, but Lyle surprised her even more.

"That's fair." He stared into her eyes without blinking. "You're right."

She opened her mouth, then quickly closed it. Caught off guard, Kam didn't know where the conversation might go next. But really, she didn't want it to go anywhere.

"I told you to leave."

"And I told you, I'm not going anywhere."

Lyle took three more steps, stopping only because he was suddenly standing right in front of her.

Kam settled deeper into the Nest, back to the sloping aluminum behind her. She couldn't smell his breath, but he was close enough to make her think she might be able to.

He was inhaling and exhaling. She was dying to hear whatever was coming.

"This thing we have together, whatever it is, it's the first real thing I've ever had in my life." He swallowed. "I'd rather be here than anywhere else in the world, if the anywhere else meant living even another minute without you. You're right, Mother *has* controlled my life. Being with you is the first real decision I've ever made from the heart, and from forehead to toe I know—"

"I don't believe you," Kam said, cutting him off with a vigorous shake of her head.

His face changed. Again. Maybe it was because it had always been one avatar to another before. This was closer than intimate, she felt like Lyle was looking inside her. Yet the penetration of his gaze was soft, like shorn grass. Far from the disgust she expected, Kam saw only concern. And not the patronizing kind that had fallen upon her like acid rain throughout a lifetime of contempt from those above her. Which was just about everyone.

Her hovel was better than being homeless, but only by a hair or so.

"Kam ..."

Her name hung in the air like a star in his sky. She didn't know how to answer. Sure, Kam knew what she wanted to say and how she longed to feel, but the risk might be too great. It would kill her if she was wrong, or if he proved that she'd been right all along.

But what if Lyle was telling the truth?

Could she ever afford to trust him?

"Why haven't you reported me?" Kam asked.

"Reported you for what?"

"For hacking eScape?"

He laughed. "You mean for doing what I wish I could do? Why would I ever want to report you for anything, especially *that*?"

"Because that's what people like you do, to people like me."

His face fell. "Then I guess you don't really know me at all."

It hurt so much, and Kam longed to take it back. But Lyle continued before she could.

"My entire life has been a play. You know those Greek theater masks?"

"Comedy and tragedy," Kam said. "Of course."

"That's been my life. For almost as long as I can remember. I've always lived on a stage, even when I wasn't actually standing on one. The performance didn't matter, and neither did the venue. I was only allowed to wear whichever mask my mother handed me, and the lines were always hers. Not just the words, but the way I said them, or moved across the stage. The whole thing has always been an act, and I can't remember not hating all of it."

"Did you ever tell her how you felt?"

"Of course! But she never listened. She would always lay right in with the guilt trip. Her words were just as scripted, but she wrote them for both of us."

"What would she say?"

"That everything she did was for me, and that I didn't appreciate all of her sacrifice and … it doesn't matter." Lyle shook his head. "Truth is, Mother has always done everything for herself. She only cares about me because of the things I can do to make her life better."

Lyle looked at her, and Kam had to keep herself from believing.

This was all too much. Exactly the kind of bullshit fairy tale she had always longed to believe. She'd been so desperate for this exact scenario — that Lyle Grace would somehow recognize her as a kindred spirit, fall in love, and take her away from this miserable life. Save Kam Landry forever, once and for all.

But that was ridiculous.

Obviously, this wasn't really happening.

Her brain had gone on the fritz. Too much Dising, or not enough.

"Kam, are you okay?"

The way Lyle was looking at her, Kam could no longer stand it.

"I need to sit."

"You are sitting," he said.

"Oh." Kam swallowed, and Lyle looked even more concerned.

He took her hands and squeezed them in his.

"I don't have much time left."

He nodded. "I know."

"Even after I upload to my new avatar, I could get nabbed by the police once inside. If they catch me, I'll be erased for good, since I don't have a body to—"

"We won't let that happen," Lyle said, squeezing her hands tighter.

Maybe Kam was comatose in the Nest and this was all in her glorious imagination.

So what? Didn't she deserve to live the fairy tale out in these scant yet quickly unspooling seconds before her death? If this was it, she might as well grab it.

Kam let go of his hands and placed hers on either side of his face.

They locked gazes, holding their stares for several long seconds.

Once she gathered her courage, Kam leaned in for a kiss.

Too much of her was still expecting him to recoil, but she surrendered with all of herself, anyway.

And to her delight and surprise, Lyle kissed her right back.

Chapter Nineteen

Lyle

LYLE COULDN'T STOP KISSING her, but he felt almost frightened to use his hands.

She seemed frail, more so than he had imagined. Not that Lyle had ever done the hard work of really thinking about it.

He gripped the Nest and kissed her harder.

Their mouths mashed together. He wasn't sure what she was feeling now. Kam had seemed so angry just a few moments before, and she was clearly still mad, or something close to it, but she was also all over him and he didn't have the strength to dissuade her.

She grabbed both sides of his collar and pulled him against her.

Lyle pulled away. "Doesn't that hurt?"

Kam answered by tugging his body toward her, thrusting her pelvis up with a moan.

They kissed for another minute before he pulled back. "Are you sure this isn't hurting you?"

"It hurts more to be away," Kam said, then glanced behind her. "The bed is softer."

Lyle stood up straight and took a step back from her Nest.

She climbed out, pointing at his pants. "A soft bed and a hard Lyle make Kam a happy girl."

"Are you sure about this?" Lyle followed her into the bedroom, looking around at a closet-sized area once inside. "Where's the bed?"

"I have to pull it out of the wall, but I don't want to." She began to undress. "So we can do it on the floor."

Lyle didn't want to take advantage of her, but watching her get undressed, that clearly wasn't what this was. She settled herself onto the floor, then looking up at Lyle with her prone yet willing body she said, "What are you waiting for?"

"Nothing," Lyle decided, getting undressed.

He slipped inside her and felt something new. There was never a river of emotion with the current flowing both ways before. Changes in tempo and rhythm were present before, but only as an expression of carnal need. They had that now, as Kam clawed her nails into his back, chewing on Lyle's neck as he held himself aloft above her body, his palms flat against the hardwood as he thrust inside her.

The sex was angry at first, or perhaps pent-up. But then it turned passionate, and in its final elegant cadence their rhythm slowed into a gently sweet release.

They climaxed as one, and for a first-timer that seemed impossible.

"You've done this before," Lyle said, rolling onto his back once they finished.

"No." She put her head on his chest and fell in time with his breathing.

Lyle was quiet. He didn't want to call Kam a liar.

Into his silence she said, "I know what you're thinking, but I've only done it in eScape. I spent a lot of time at Bros."

"Seriously?"

She laughed. "Unlimited sessions. Another hacker advantage. Want me to book you some time at Broads?"

"Not at all." Lyle shook his head. "I only want you for the rest of my life."

"You don't mean that."

"I do," he said.

But Kam didn't respond. Or maybe she *wouldn't.* Despite what they had just done, she seemed resistant to hearing, as if making a hearty effort to disbelieve him. Her entire body was blushing, and her glow suggested joy, but her eyes were far off and he could swear she was ever slowly inching away.

"What are you thinking?"

"I'm enjoying the silence," she said.

"That's not an answer. I want to know what you're thinking about … right now."

"You only think that's what you want."

"Just stop it, Kam. Why do you do that? I know what I want, and right now that's for you to tell me the truth, no matter what that might be."

She sighed, then fell silent. But this time Lyle didn't press her. He could hear her thinking, slowly turning the words before she finally let them out of her mouth to cut the quiet between them.

"You've been a fantasy of mine for a long time," she finally admitted.

The revelation wasn't exactly surprising, but still it filled Lyle with a warm glow. He pulled her against him and waited for Kam to continue.

"*Lyle Grace.*" She said his name like an incantation.

"Thinking about you was the only way I could ever get through those seminars. I imagined something like this, but only as a daydream. It was never something I ever, ever *ever* really believed."

He wanted to say something like, *Well, you should have*, but that would only make Kam feel like he wasn't really hearing her.

She saw only the poverty and believed it made her repulsive. But in truth he couldn't care less. Lyle couldn't help what he had been born into, and neither could she.

"I wish we met a long time ago." It felt like the safest thing to say.

"We did. You just don't remember me."

At least she didn't say what Lyle knew she was probably thinking: *Because I wasn't worth remembering.*

"I'm glad I was a fantasy of yours. Now you're all of mine."

Kam blushed harder. "You don't mean that."

"I can't wait to explore all of you, once you're finally uploaded."

The ensuing silence was heavy; he couldn't bear to break it.

"I'm not sure that's going to happen," she finally admitted.

"What do you mean?" Lyle asked, rolling away from her.

"I might be too far gone. Even if—"

"There must be something we can do … something *I can do*. Just tell me what you need. I'll do anything—"

"It's not that simple."

"How do you know? Do you need a doctor? Drugs? Someone who can help with the code? A different Nest?" A ray of hope, piercing his chest. "I can take you to my place and you can use my—"

A loud knock on Kam's front door, coming from the other room.

Lyle looked at her, but she appeared as confused as he felt.

"Are you expecting anyone?"

She shook her head and he wanted to curse himself. Mother had followed him, or had him tracked. Of course she found him and was now outside the door. Of course Lyle had been a big enough idiot to lead her here.

"I'm so sorry." He stood and started putting on his pants.

"For what?"

Lyle left the room without an answer, shirtless on his way to the front door.

He peeked out through a filthy window expecting to see Mother, but instead he saw a tiny woman in an absurd-looking trench coat and fedora that he immediately recognized from outside the Hotel Bisou during that ambush with Miley.

He flung open the door and yelled, "You need to get the hell out of here!"

"Connie Bledsoe, with *The Daily Fink*. I just have a couple of questions. If you can—"

"I'm not talking to anyone from *The Daily Fink*," Lyle said.

"Who is it?" Kam asked, now fully dressed and standing behind him.

"A vulture. But don't worry, it'll be gone soon."

"I'm sorry, Mr. Grace," said Connie Bledsoe from *The Daily Fink*, "but this is a public street and under Communication Accord 631 I have every right to camp out here, and I'll be exercising that right until you decide to—"

Lyle slammed the door and turned to Kam. "We're going to have to sneak out. This place have a back door?

She laughed. "You're kidding, right? No, there's no back door, but there is a window to the alley. We can climb out, assuming there's not another reporter waiting out there."

"I'm sure we can lose her once we get to my car. Same for anyone else who might try and follow us. We can finish the upload in my Nest. What do you need to—"

"I'll handle the tech. Can you gather my meds?"

"Of course," Lyle said, then listened as she gave him directions before repeating them back to her.

A minute later he was packing everything exactly as she instructed. He glanced over to where Kam was gathering her assorted gear at just the wrong moment. He saw her closing a window on-screen and wished he'd seen nothing instead. He wanted to ask her what it was, but he already knew, and the sight made him sick to his stomach.

Kam looked over at him. Lyle smiled, fast as he could find it. He needed to bury the uncertainty, now clotting like blood in his veins. He could tell by her expression, she wanted to know if he'd seen it. The projection was only there for a second. A flash as she closed the window. But even in that moment he saw enough. The image swallowed the wall with what looked like a crazy shrine dedicated to him.

You've been a fantasy of mine for a long time.

The words felt different, now with this wall of context.

Old doubts percolated to the surface, more belligerent for having been shoved to the back of his mind.

Had Kam been stalking him this entire time?

Could he really ever believe a single thing she had to say?

Lyle wasn't just the subject of her vision board, seeing it like that made him feel like a target.

He offered her another friendly nod and kept packing

the medicine. Once she was far enough away for him to feel sure she was out of earshot, he muttered in his lowest voice.

"*Vox* ..."

Yes, his assistant answered immediately.

"I need you to grab as much of Kam's data as you can, and pull it from any available stream."

You mean you need me to steal it.

"Whatever. Just do your job."

I hardly think—

"Just do it," Lyle growled.

"I'm sorry?" Kam called from across the room.

"Nothing. Just talking to myself." Doubting her felt like a crown of thorns on his soul. But there was nothing he could do. The thoughts were there, refusing to leave.

Was she really a gold digger?

Had he fallen for some sort of seduction scam?

And worst of all, was Kam crazy like her father?

"Ready?" Kam asked.

He wasn't sure. Vox hadn't reported back and Lyle wasn't sure if he should stall for more time. Was hacking servers and databases like a conversation, slowed for the benefit of human perception? Or did he really need the time to save Lyle from himself?

"Ready," he finally answered.

Kam climbed out the window first. She gave the all-clear — no reporters in the alley — then Lyle followed behind.

"We need the car," he said to Vox.

But the Valkyrie was already rolling up.

They were getting in as Connie Bledsoe came running after the vehicle.

The engine roared, then they raced into the street.

The cabin was silent as Lyle kept his focus on the road.

The car was driving itself, but he wanted to appear deep in thought.

But he didn't need to worry. Kam was spent. Just two minutes on the road and her head had already lolled to the side, passed out from exhaustion.

She never saw Connie Bledsoe, driving like a maniac behind them, surely filming every second of their pursuit.

Chapter Twenty

Kam

KAM OPENED her eyes with the feel of a cool sheet kissing her skin and no idea where she was.

She sat up in bed and looked around. If it wasn't the Bisou, it wanted to be. The room was the creamiest thing she'd ever seen, from the sheets, to the silken couch, to a black box full of cascading Phalaenopsis orchids, with blush-colored throats spilling down from the lid of an all-white Steinway.

Who needed a grand piano in their hotel room?

Maybe it wasn't real. Or maybe this wasn't a hotel room at all.

What if she was in Lyle's house right now, and a dream come true was even truer?

"Where is he?" Kam asked Pibly, since she was apparently alone.

Lyle Grace did not say where he was going.

"Any guesses?" Then: "And how long has he been gone?"

He might have gone to get food. He has been gone for about fifteen minutes.

"Where are we, and how long have we been here?"

You're at the Chateau Bleu, and you've been here for around two hours.

"Great." Kam didn't like the idea of being unconscious for a couple of hours while Lyle had the chance to sit there and stare at her. "Did he look at me? While I was out, I mean?"

She felt weak for asking, but it wasn't like the AI was going to judge her.

A little, Pibly told her. *But he was also interested in something else.*

"What?" Kam asked.

Mr. Grace had his assistant access your workstation while you were unconscious.

"He can do that?"

Her heart was pounding, knowing what he'd already seen, the flickering projection that used an entire wall to broadcast her infatuation with Lyle back at her shithole apartment.

He can and has.

Worse than betrayed, Kam felt embarrassed. She could only think of two reasons why Lyle would go poking through her data. Either he didn't trust her, or he planned on turning her in to the police. Maybe both.

"Is anything missing?"

No. Nothing is missing.

"Is anything copied?"

Several hundred files.

"Like?"

More specifically, all the files from within the Lyle Grace folder.

She swallowed hard, wanting to cry.

Kam could only imagine what that must look like, to

see all of those files out of context. She'd already admitted to fantasizing about him for most of her life, but now Lyle would know it was something more. Like an unrelenting obsession.

Kam could say adios to any help he had been willing to offer. Maybe she should bail, get out of the room before he came back. Her current avatar and the new version were both ready to go. If she could find a Nest to borrow, there was no reason Kam couldn't upload herself right now. She could start over and Lyle would never be able to find her.

Unless he traced her identity through the Nest's last upload.

He had the resources to hunt her down inside eScape. But did he even want to? Or after seeing her shrine of insanity would Lyle finally be done with her?

"Where's the nearest publicly available Nest?"

There are three available in this hotel. But none accept eScape credits and all are outside your price range. And not by a little. They're—

"You don't need to rub it in, I got it. Where is the nearest publicly available Nest that also accepts eScape credits?"

Three blocks from here, at eScape Cafe. There are currently seven open units.

"Great." Kam began to get out of bed.

Unfortunately, there has been additional degradation to your brain making a full upload presently impossible.

"What? Why? Because I lost consciousness?"

Sex requires quite a lot of processing power, even when operating under optimum conditions.

"Great. So what am I supposed to do?"

You need several more doses of Dising before you can upload yourself.

"I can't afford any more Dising. Are you sure I don't

have enough with what's left? Can we get any in exchange for eScape credits?"

You know that regulations prohibit that. You have enough to make one final visit to eScape, if you choose to spend the rest of what will be a very short life trapped inside your failing body.

"Great."

Kam didn't say anything else, and Pibly didn't prompt her. She didn't know what to do, and didn't really want to do anything. She felt crushed, barely felt the will to live. It was her time, and maybe that was fine. Life had never been much worth living, and she would have been a fool to expect that to change, especially now at the end.

She had probably lost all hope of getting Lyle's help, and too bad because she had no way in hell of filling a Dising prescription without it. Her Hail Mary now was one last visit to eScape. After that it was either a choice of logging out to die in the real world, or hanging out inside the artificial one, waiting until her body could no longer sustain the Deep Spell.

Kam didn't know what would happen after that. No one did, because no one had ever returned from dying to tell the story. She might disappear, glitch, or become a glitch in the system.

There's something you need to see.

"What is it?" Kam asked Pibly, coming out of her reverie.

The far wall lit up with a broadcast.

Another news story to maul her broken heart.

Kam read the ticker at the bottom of the screen a split-second before the anchor opened her mouth. The ticker read, *Baker Grace, father of self-help guru Lyle Grace, hangs himself in his hotel room.*

Audio boomed through the room as the anchor finished her sentence with a smile.

"—it read, 'I've been waiting for years, and now reuniting with Lyle has made my life complete.' The note also said, 'Now that it's finally happened, it is my wish to go quietly into that good night.'" The anchor smiled for the camera. "The full text of his suicide note can be found online at …"

Kam's heart was holding most of her weight. But regardless of what Lyle thought of her, she had to make sure he was okay before she left the world forever.

She couldn't stand the thought of this tragedy with his father leading him back into Julia's arms.

Chapter Twenty-One

Lyle

LYLE STARED at the screen in disbelief.

He couldn't tell if his heart was pounding, or if it had stopped beating altogether.

The anchor looked into the camera, reading the teleprompter with words that shook his life at the edges.

"Authorities found a suicide note, confirmed to be written by Baker Grace himself. It read, 'I've been waiting for years, and now reuniting with Lyle has made my life complete.' The note also said, 'Now that it's finally happened, it is my wish to go quietly into that good night.'" The anchor smiled, practically grinned, as though this was all such excellent news. "The full text of his suicide note can be found online at our website, on our news app, or at any of our hubs within eScape ..."

"Turn it off," Lyle said to Vox.

Of course. I just thought you should know.

Lyle supposed the AI was right, but now he had no idea what to do with the information. He was depressed enough, logged into eScape, still a slave to Mother and unable to stop himself from thinking about Kam for more than a few seconds at a time. Lyle had agreed to something he already regretted, not just leaving his girlfriend (that wasn't the right word, was it?) alone to meet Mother at the giant digital venue where she planned to give some of their biggest fans a preview of her new couples healing program, first broadcast throughout eScape to early birds in attendance, then to the world.

But now Lyle was sweating even more than before. His dad was dead, and the cool sweat on his neck insisted the same things as his dry mouth and clammy hands: Mother had something to do with this; of course she did.

I'm done with the business, Mother. For the rest of my life, I'm done with Ruthlessly Positive, and if you're not willing to let me go, then I'm sorry, but I'm done with you, too.

Lyle rehearsed the same set of words he'd been turning around in his head for a while now, but after hearing the poisonous news from an overzealous anchor, they were now coming easier.

He poured himself a tall glass of water, then gulped it dry, fast enough to give himself hiccups.

Lyle set the empty glass on a table, looking up at the now dark wall, wondering if the brewing emotion he felt for Mother had finally found its way to hate, or maybe something even worse.

He took out his phone and swiped over to the script Mother had sent over right after he logged into eScape. She made him promise to read it, but he'd barely glanced at the thing. He certainly hadn't bothered to learn his lines. Lyle kept telling himself that he wasn't going to partici-pate. The entire time he was looking for Kam, leaving Elysium for the city's darkest and dingiest corners, seeing it all from behind the wheel of an Aston Martin while making a promise to himself that he'd finally tell his mother off. Insist that she was on her own with this next product, then every one that would follow for the rest of her goddamned life.

He hadn't read the script, because Lyle was still telling himself that he wouldn't go through with it. He still had every intention of parting ways with her. Still willing to leave without looking back. But things had changed so much, and in barely any time. Kam was dying and his dad was already dead. Lyle had planned to leave Mother so he could build a new life away from her with Kam at his side, but now that future had fallen away from him.

The prospect of going through with it alone was a horror. Worse than the clammy hands and dry mouth, Lyle's stomach kept feeling sicker. He was nauseous. Even a slow walk made him want to vomit.

But he couldn't stay here in his dressing room, pretending to rehearse while waiting for Mother to finish ruining his life.

He poured himself another glass of water, downed it even faster than the first, then pressed a palm to his stomach while waiting for the next wave of nausea to pass. He swallowed once, then gathered his courage and marched out of the room.

I'm done with the business, Mother. For the rest of my life, I'm done with Ruthlessly Positive, and if you're not willing to let me go, then I'm sorry, but I'm also done with you.

He made his way down the hall, still rehearsing the words in his head, walking faster with every step, thickening his valor like a snowball gathering size and speed on its way down the hill.

He was out of rehearsal now, this was the real deal: Lyle was about to tell his mother off, once and for all. He would say the words that were long overdue, finally vent everything he'd been forced to bottle inside before leaving Mother to her toxic disfunction forever.

The dressing room door was closed, but Lyle barely even stopped in front of it. He didn't knock, or check to see if it was locked. Instead, he swung it wide and barreled inside.

Mother's assistant, Harmony, was the only one to look up at him. Mother was inspecting her nails. She could get oddly particular about their look, and thanks to the infinite options, all available at the speed of thought within eScape, she usually tried several dozen before settling on her favorite, especially when it was time to sell something new.

"Did you murder my father?" Lyle asked without preamble, not caring that Harmony was present, hoping it would humiliate the woman who pretended to give when she only knew how to take.

But it didn't. Instead she looked up from her nails with a rancorous smile. "Harmony, would you be so kind as to check in with the live feeds and make sure our subscribers in tiers one through three were all informed?"

"Of course, Ms. Grace." Harmony smiled with a tiny bow before she scurried from the room, heeding his mother's ridiculous request. Whether she was "checking in with the live feeds" or "making sure their subscribers were informed," either task could have been accomplished on Harmony's tablet, since in reality she was sitting in her own Nest back in Mother's offices.

"Did you kill my father, or not?" Lyle asked, the second Harmony closed the door behind her.

"Of course I did," Mother said, holding her smile.

He'd assumed she'd start with a denial, then filibuster her way into Lyle believing her. This was unexpected.

"You shouldn't be surprised. It was the right thing to

do, and entirely your fault. You should thank me for taking care of the problem."

"I should be *thanking you*? And how is this *my fault*?"

"You knew what you were doing, using your father to get away from me."

Lyle stared in disbelief, not just at how casually his mom was admitting to murder, with obvious pride pulling at the corners of her mouth.

He shook his head, but only a lone syllable left his mouth.

"No …"

"Oh yes, Lyle. Whether you like it or not, this is very much *your fault*. You should have turned your father away, instead of giving him ideas. He wanted more money. And not just one payment — he was demanding a percentage of everything we do together in exchange for his silence. Does that sound reasonable to you?"

He shook his head. "I can't believe you."

"It's not hard to believe, Lyle. You've lived with me long enough to understand my rules."

"You're not even pretending anymore … you're sick."

"I'm quite well, and no, I'm not pretending. I don't see how that would serve either one of us right now." Mother grinned again, her most malignant smile so far. "It's better to treat this situation with as much Ruthless Positivity as we can, don't you think?"

"No, I don't, and this isn't my fault! I'm done with the guilt trips and with you." Lyle paused for a beat before he finally blurted his rehearsal: "I'm done with the business, Mother. For the rest of my life, I'm done with Ruthlessly Positive, and if you're not willing to let me go, then I'm sorry, but I'm also done with you."

Mother laughed. "You can't be done, Lyle. Not now, or ever. You will always be my little boy."

He shook his head. "I'm not your little boy anymore, and I never will be again. You can't make me do anything I don't want to do. Those days are gone for—"

"Do you have any idea what it's like to live in this world without money?"

"I don't give a shit about the money anymore. You can—"

"Oh, you will."

"—keep your fucking trust."

Her eyes widened in surprise. "How dare you swear at me. Your father made that same mistake, you know. It was the last one he ever made."

Through gritted teeth Lyle said, "You can't control me."

Mother laughed again. "Is that what you think?"

He stared, trying to read her expression and the reptilian mirth that appeared to be fueling it.

"The cocktail I used to make your father behave was never perfect, but a lot of progress has been made in the last eighteen years. The drugs these days are quite impressive. More direct with fewer side effects." She smiled even wider, then leaned forward and finished with a pair of words that left her mouth in barely more than a whisper. "*You'll see.*"

"Log out now," Lyle said to Vox.

But his AI didn't respond.

The panic was icy and cold and immediate.

Lyle understood exactly what was happening, and just how neatly he had fallen in line with his mother's scheming. She would drug her son with Estravir to keep him in line. He needed to flee eScape. He'd been inside too long already anyway. He needed to check on Kam, and save himself from—

"There's nothing to worry about, Lyle. Doctor Bryant

has assured me that you'll be happy, assuming you can find the inner wisdom to accept what's happening, and embrace the opportunity for what it is."

"No …" Lyle shook his head in disbelief, a broken argument leaving his lips in shambles. "I'm done with the business … for the rest of my life … I'm done with Ruthlessly Positive … and—"

"If I'm not willing to let you go, then you're also done with me?"

She took one last look at her nails, then left Lyle alone in the room, locking the door behind her. There was nothing he could do to escape, not now or ever. Mother had total control of the permissions.

"Vox," he called to the empty room. "Please, are you there?"

But Lyle was alone. Worse, he was trapped.

And still, the biggest thought in his head, and one that wouldn't stop looping.

Is Kam going to be okay?

Chapter Twenty-Two

Kam

AGAIN, Pibly continued with yet another warning Kam had no interest in hearing, let alone heeding, *I must warn you that the danger of*—

"Nothing has changed in the last five minutes, right?" Kam didn't give her assistant even a second to answer. "Of course it hasn't, so let's agree that I already understand the risks."

Pibly buzzed in the background. Faint, as though the sound was bleeding up from the base of her skull, processing, the AI working to determine whether it should go ahead and override her last orders. Maybe save the stupid human from herself.

No, this wasn't exactly her smartest move ever, but she had little choice. It was bad enough waking up in that hotel all alone. The place was nice, but without Lyle around and nearing the end of her sentence, the room felt more like a prison than anything.

Then the news about Lyle's father. Of course Julia had

something to do with it. There was evil in that woman's eyes. So yes, it was a risk, uploading herself to eScape for what could very well be her final time. It was a good enough place to die, a hell of a lot better than the real-world misery waiting outside of it.

Maybe she'd never see it again. And if so, good riddance.

Kam walked three blocks from the hotel to eScape Cafe, but that might as well have been a half-marathon. She was out of breath by the time she checked in, enough so that the manager didn't want to rent her a Nest. She threw a fit, and after it looked like that might not work, Kam demanded an audience with the owner. She offered him ten thousand eScape credits to let her log on.

What did she care? She would have offered more, but her gut screamed that another credit would tip her over the edge. An owner willing to bend the law might call on it instead, figuring if this ragged girl was offering that much, then surely someone else would be willing to offer more. But ten grand made for a nice round number that an enterprising man like the owner of eScape Cafe might want to keep invisible.

Now Kam was sitting in a Nest, all the way in back of the Cafe, contemplating her avatars. She wasn't sure which of the two at her disposal she should use. The old one would make it easier for Lyle to see her, in case she didn't spot him first. But the new one might be smarter.

Kam wished she could trust him. The little life she had left inside eScape needed to be lived under the radar, and it would be easier to avoid getting spotted if she was wearing the new one. But if for some miracle Kam was able to get her hands on more Dising, then the new avatar made a lot more sense.

She had to keep asking herself, *What do I believe?*

A part of her was hoping that Lyle had forgiven her, at least enough to help her out. She hated the mercenary voice in her head, insisting that even if Lyle refused to grant her emotional amnesty, he might be willing to give her what she needed to ensure both her absence and silence.

After an embarrassing amount of deliberation, feeling sands like rain in a life-sized hourglass, Kam finally logged onto eScape with her new avatar and found herself face-to-face with an instant surprise.

Lyle wasn't done with his mother at all. The two of them would be taking the stage together for a "very special event" at the Crystal Cathedral. She hoped the seminar's name embarrassed him: *Mutually Ruthless.*

Pure fury snaked through her body, the rage of betrayal like lava bubbling over the lip of a frothing volcano. Kam didn't understand what he was doing, but worse, she couldn't comprehend what they had shared. Her body was running on empty, and that turned sex into surrender. She had given what little she had left to Lyle, handed it over with faith. But he snatched Kam's gift like an hors d'oeuvre off of a silver tray passing in front of him.

She stared up at the sign for Mutually Ruthless, fixed to the lavish all-glass cathedral, then drew a deeply needed breath before crossing the street, smiling at the doorperson as she entered the building.

That's as far as she made it. Anyone could enter the cathedral, but only those with tickets could breach the amphitheater. She walked to one of the many kiosks scattered throughout the lobby, swiped her payment information into the system, upgraded herself to the front section (though nothing was available in the front row at any price), then waited for the ding to let her know the request for a single VIP pass had been approved.

She took another breath, each one felt stolen by now, then made her way toward the orchestra pit, smiling at all the beautifully dressed people as she passed them by, wondering if she would see any of her old friends. Or at least the annoying prima donna socialites she once pretended to like, so she could keep the iciest tendrils of loneliness out of her decaying body.

She planned to pass the orchestra pit and head directly backstage. Her VIP passes were for the meet-and-greet that followed the seminar. Kam would feign ignorance if caught, but she needed to see Lyle immediately, and couldn't stomach an hour or more of Julia Grace and her merciless platitudes, or the way she would be playing puppet master to her son.

But she didn't make it far. Kam pulled out her phone, preparing to show her ticket to the doorperson, when she heard a familiar voice calling out from behind her. The last one in the world she wanted to hear.

"Kam?"

"I'm sorry?" She turned around, calling Julia's bluff. There was no way she could really know who Kam was. The woman was obviously guessing. "Oh my God, you're Julia Grace!"

"Cut the shit, sweetheart. I know who you are, and I know why you're here."

"I'm here to learn more about being Mutually Ruthless," Kam replied with a cold stare that clashed with the artifice in her overheated smile. "I can't wait to see what the two of you are going to share! You know, I've been coming to your seminars ever since I was a little girl."

"Yes, with your loser father. I wish I could say I remember, but you were never important enough. I had to look it up."

Kam swallowed and tried not to choke. "My father is the curator at—"

"Your father died like the lunatic he was."

"You're a snake oil-selling thief!"

"You might want to keep your voice down." Julia took an extra beat to prove her unwavering calm. "Not for my benefit, of course. Anyone here has surely heard all the usual arguments. But unless you want security to escort you out immediately, I would really keep it down."

Julia smiled: *your move.*

Quieter, but not at all quiet, Kam said, "You tell your customers that everything that happens to them is *their fault.* That if someone wants to improve their life, they have to 'ruthlessly root out every negative thing in their psyche and replace it with something positive.'"

Julia gave her a mocking, derisive laugh. "Are you applying to be a Ruthlessly Positive Certified Coach? I'm sure you could learn the material, but I don't know how believable you'd be. Plus, you'll be dead soon, and what good will you be to anyone then? Except to me, because dead means you're out of my hair."

"Say someone gets hit by a drunk driver and they end up in a wheelchair for life?" Kam continued, unfazed. "You're really saying they manifested that by harboring negativity? What lesson is someone supposed to learn from getting paralyzed?"

"That letting go of negative feelings about being trapped in a wheelchair could make that person a beacon of inspirational positivity for the rest of the disabled community."

"You're rewarding people for repressing unhappiness and pretending to love their lives."

Julia offered her another serpentine smile. "I've read

that criticism before. It's always written by someone who is clearly miserable."

"You use your son as a sales tool."

"Of course I do. He's the best one I have."

"You use a shaming-through-positive-thinking approach to help parents raise their children."

"It's highly effective."

"I'm here to tell you, it's broken."

"No, Kam Landry. *You* are broken. You have no power here, and you never will. I have known Lyle for every second of the life that I gave him. You've known him for a relative hour, and he doesn't know you at all. Lyle thinks he's sly, but I know every move he makes. He thinks he can fool me with his silly little surveillance-blocking apps, but anyone with money can pay to get around them. I know when he eats and when he masturbates. I know what his brainwave profile looks like when he sleeps, when he's attracted to a seminar attendee, and when he lies and says he's walking to the corner store in order to log onto his silly little secret Nest that he thinks I'm foolish enough to not know about."

"You can't—"

"So here's what's going to happen …" Julia continued, not raising her voice or sharpening her tone, yet still somehow sounding as though she owned every word in the world. "I'm going to call security, and you're going to let them quietly escort you out. Then you're going to stay away from us forever."

"Why would I ever do that?"

"Because I'm going to find it in my heart to help you."

"You mean pay me off?"

"You're a lost cause, always focusing on the negatives instead of the positives. You deserve your misery, but that won't stop me from putting this to bed in the way that serves us both. The second you're gone from the premises I will send you a one-time payment. Those funds will allow you to live well for the rest of your short life. And properly doped up, so maybe you can smile some in the real world during the remainder of your miserable existence."

"And if I refuse, are you going to have me killed like Baker Grace?"

Julia smiled. "Even if you weren't half dead, a girl like you will never get a better offer. Last chance."

"How did you know? That it was me in this avatar?"

Julia shrugged, as if her answer meant nothing. "Connie Bledsoe told me enough to find out the rest. Lyle was stupid enough to bring you back to a hotel where I have eyes. He really should have known better after what happened at the Hotel Bisou."

Kam had to agree, but wouldn't give Julia the satisfaction of doing so out loud.

"I had you followed from the hotel to eScape Cafe, and the owner was happy to show me to your Nest after I promised that he could keep your little candy credits, in addition to my offer of genuine credits he could spend in the real world however he wanted to."

Julia leaned close enough that her breath mingled with the waft of perfume. "Face it, sweetheart, you never stood a chance."

"You can't buy me." Then Kam took a chance. "And you can't buy Lyle."

Julia laughed, long and miserable, each cackling slicing into Kam's skin like the tip of a knife. "I've taken care of Lyle already, and if you give me any more trouble, I'll take care of you, too. *Last chance.*"

"You already said that."

Julia whispered, "*Security.*"

But Kam was already gone.

Chapter Twenty-Three

Lyle

LYLE PICKED UP THE CHAIR, hurled it against the mirror, then watched the glass crack into webbing before falling into shards in the carpet.

Then he exhaled, watching as the scene reset itself, same as it had every other time before.

His purgatory was rigged, and no matter what he did, there wasn't any escape. He'd ripped the room apart several times already, his hopes for any exit dimming a bit with every fresh attempt. It was futile and he knew it, but Lyle couldn't let that stop him from trying.

He called for security, screamed for them over and over and over. He pounded on the walls and the door, crying out for anyone who might be able to hear him. Lyle didn't have many friends in the real world, and even fewer in eScape. Even if he did, there was no one to call. Mother had done something to the room's permissions. Every contact was gone from his phone, and everything he tried just reset itself a few seconds later.

He picked up the chair, hurled it against the mirror, then watched the glass crack into webbing before falling into shards in the carpet.

Once the chair was back in place, Lyle sat on it hard.

This wasn't the end. He would find a way out, along with a path back to Kam.

Maybe he shouldn't be sitting. Staying in one place made it even harder to keep from freaking out. And that was already feeling impossible. Because Lyle was sure he knew what Mother was doing. She would somehow coerce him into the seminar, with enough of a performance to build a lasting buzz. Then she'd take him offline and out of eScape, where Dr. Bryant would shoot him up with a supposedly new and improved version of the drugs that had destroyed his father's brain.

He had to keep that from happening, but Lyle didn't know how. He was a prisoner until Mother decided otherwise. That truth made it hard to bar his avalanche of thoughts. He saw himself as a zombie without volition, wandering around without direction, forever at his mother's beck and call, her every wish his obligated command.

Dead might be better than living the rest of his life in a daze designed by her.

Lyle stood from his chair. Then he picked it up, hurled it against the mirror, still exhaling as the scene reset itself with the usual show.

There had to be a way out of this, and he would find it.

Worst case scenario, he would ambush her on-stage, scream a truth to the world she would never expect. Except, of course she would. Mother had been a step ahead of Lyle for his entire life — what made today any different?

Maybe there was hope. Maybe the Estravir wouldn't

have the same side effects they had with his father. It wasn't in Mother's best interests for him to completely fade away.

Lyle's charm moved a lot of product. Neuter that and she might be hobbling an entire limb of the business. She would probably keep him just numb enough, to live a long and healthy live by her side as a slave.

Lyle wanted to scream. So he did, but no one came running.

He screamed again. Threw his chair against the mirror. Cursed his mother for being the monster she was. Expected her to storm in and demand an apology. Hoped she would so he could bash her fucking skull in.

No, he shook himself out of it.

Thoughts like that were letting her win.

What if he ended up as a vegetable? The horror of his life might be even worse than the atrocities he could already imagine, a marionette to his mother.

He had to do something, but the *what* still hadn't materialized. There was no way to do anything in this place, not in the parts controlled by Julia Grace. She must have turned the room soundproof or something, because the walls were relatively thin and he'd been hearing the crowds outside for a while. Excitement was swelling, but despite his curdling screams, no one had answered his cries.

Lyle considered trying again, but he didn't have the energy. It took too much out of him. Right now, he didn't even have the muster to hurl his chair against the mirror. He felt plastered to the seat, paralyzed in contemplation, for the first time considering this wicked trap his witch mother had set for him.

A new thought dawned, even worse than the rest of them:

What if she never let him leave eScape?

Was that a fate worse than death?

It was one thing to control him in the outside world. Even drugged, Mother would have to spend her life wondering if things were going according to plan. Lyle could figure out a way to trick her into thinking he was taking his pills; someone might see what was happening and reach out to help him; he could maybe develop a tolerance to Estravir and the lessening effects would help him figure out a way to eScape.

But breaking free was impossible inside eScape, and keeping him trapped in her personal eternity was simply a matter of setting permissions.

What would it be like, to live here forever. Mother would do her best to ply him with surface confections. Food and alcohol, rooms full of women all waiting to please him. Whatever he wanted whenever he wanted it, so long as it happened in here, and he never failed to follow his orders.

But Mother would never allow Lyle to have any real friends, or true connections. She would see anyone who ever cared about him as a threat to be dealt with.

He stood, turned his chair away from the mirror, then sat back down and stared at the taupe-colored wall, hating this room and all the artifice inside it.

He screamed, then screamed again, unsettled by his quickly creeping panic.

Another new thought, this one somehow worse.

Lyle wondered if he had already been given drugs in the real world, and that was the cause for his sudden alarm. Klaxons screamed between his ears, but maybe there was a reason.

If Mother had given him the drugs, then it was too late already.

He was under her spell, here in eScape *and* out there in

the real world. Trapped in his Nest, where she promised him that everything would be better.

Lyle never should have believed her lies.

Now he'd ruined it for himself and for Kam.

Her name was an icepick at his throat. Mother had been ahead of him this entire time, so she was probably onto Kam. He hadn't wanted to think about that, but now he couldn't help it. Images of her discovery flooded his mind. Mother knowing which hotel they were at because he'd been foolish enough to be brazen.

What would she do at her worst? Trap Kam in eScape, same as him? Maybe Mother would offer him what she saw as a pet in exchange for her compliance.

But no, she would never show such a kindness, even as misdirected as it would be.

Lyle couldn't afford to just sit here. He needed a plan.

He had been giving Mother too much credit. Sure, she controlled the permissions in this room, and perhaps everywhere in the Cathedral if she'd paid for the pleasure. But Mother didn't own eScape, and if Lyle could get out of this place and onto the street, his odds of getting out of this situation would explode.

He could save himself, and Kam.

He had the wrong idea before, thinking he could out her onstage. That was the measured response she had trained into him, but it made more sense to run. Time had turned sloppy, and Lyle didn't know how long she'd left him locked inside this room. She would need him for the seminar, and soon.

But he wouldn't bolt when she opened the door. She might expect such an attempt, and Lyle was smart enough to understand that he had exactly one chance. He wasn't willing to waste it down a long and vacant hallway, while everyone was seated and waiting for him to take the stage. Instead, Lyle would wait until he was in front of the crowd. Then he could sprint into the audience and get lost in the masses, where it would be much harder for Mother to see or follow or exercise any more of her inappropriate and surely illegal control.

It was a mother-and-son performance. She couldn't run this seminar without him. He had to wait, and be ready to make his move at the first opportunity.

But his chance would never come.

The empty wall brightened with a billion pixels, the taupe now gone in favor of a screen. He watched with an open mouth as Mother took the stage to thunderous applause.

The Mutually Ruthless Seminar had started without him.

Fruitless as it was, Lyle stood and picked up his chair.

He turned around, hurled it against the mirror, then sat on the floor, watching the glass dissolve into shards in the carpet before resetting itself.

Then Lyle closed his eyes, hoping with all of his heart that Kam was safe.

Chapter Twenty-Four

Kam

KAM DIDN'T FEEL SAFE.

She must look ridiculous to anyone paying attention, the way she kept glancing over her shoulder at every crossed street and intersection, darting from one knot of shadows to the next, knowing with every dash that even ditching her pursuers didn't mean she could outrun the paranoia itself.

It was a sober realization: Kam could never be free of the tracking or trailing. Julia would make her miserable for whatever life she had left. There was no being free of the luxury huckster. She would never really pay Kam off to keep her invisible, but she would surely be happy to purchase enough time to make her comfortable, to lower Kam's guard and expose her naked throat.

Not that she would be so brazen as to slice it with a knife. Julia was more subtle, which was why her strain of evil often stayed invisible. At first Kam merely suspected, but she had peered into the woman's eyes and now knew exactly what kind of woman she was. Julia would have her killed without flinching — make it look like Kam had died of a disease that would have finished her off in a few weeks anyway, just because she didn't want to wait that long to enjoy her peace of mind.

She would do anything to see Lyle. Needed it like fresh air after an afternoon in the sulfur mines. Not that she was a baby in want of his comfort. Quite the opposite: Kam felt an overwhelming need to make sure he was safe. Even if she could only see Lyle on stage next to his evil bitch of a mother, that would be enough for now. She just needed some sort of inkling that he was okay.

Another three knotted tangles of shadow and Kam found herself turning onto a wider street from the clogged artery of a narrow alleyway, congested with bags of garbage and abandoned, broken-down vehicles. Kam approached a public kiosk, logged in, and immediately felt the clock ticking.

Julia knew the identity of her new avatar. If she was having Kam's activity within eScape tracked — and of course she was — then Kam's time was running out already.

Kam swiped until she found the right feed. A livestream of the Mutually Ruthless Seminar from inside eScape. Julia was pacing the stage alone, making eyes for the camera and talking about the success of Ruthless Positivity as a mindset, now through the filter of what she called "permanent partnership."

Julia stopped and looked out into the audience. But to Kam it felt like she was staring directly at her as she spoke.

"This next phase of the Ruthlessly Positive System is a long time coming, and for those of you who have been needing it the most in their lives, long overdue. Our apologies that it's taken us this long, but this was something Lyle and I had to get right."

Julia paused, giving her audience a long moment, steeping in the trust she insisted forever flowed in both directions during every seminar.

"What I'm about to share is the most complicated part of what Lyle and I have spent his life developing. I'm proud of my son for embracing this important work, and inheriting the responsibility of changing the world with positivity. But my son is also smart enough to understand that this isn't the sort of work he could ever accomplish all on his own, and that he needs a different kind of partner for this next phase of his journey."

Kam's heart hammered against her ribcage.

Julia's plan was peeling back at the edges, but there still wasn't enough for Kam to identify the breed of evil buried underneath.

She'd been at the kiosk for five minutes.

That might be four too long. Even dying to hear what Julia was about to say next, Kam had to get the hell out of here.

"There is an unparalleled power in having someone love you for who you are, despite your imperfections and—"

She logged out, made an about-face from the kiosk, and darted back into the shadows.

She waited, not surprised to see a tall man enter the clearing, looking down both sides of the street before turning to the kiosk with disappointment etched in his expression.

Kam was rotting inside, wondering where Lyle was, knowing he needed her and that there might be nothing she could do, and no way to save him.

But then, crouched in the shadows, she had an idea.

It was dangerous, and Kam didn't know what might happen if she got caught. But still, it was worth the risk. Of course, she knew where Lyle lived. If Kam could find a way inside Elysium, then she maybe she could even the odds. Information was the most important weapon at her disposal, and she needed to know more than she did, which right now was uncomfortably close to nothing.

Lyle's posh neighborhood was all the way across town. A FASTr would require more credits than she should reasonably spend on a ride, but seeing as this was the end of everything, Kam figured *fuck it*, and dropped a third of her credits so she could move from crumbling boulevards to manicured lawns in the shortest amount of time possible.

THE FASTR LEFT her in front of the Elysium gates, and Kam felt grateful she'd been delivered in a driverless car. No one ever *needed* a driver, but the Fair Employment Act required that every company had its fair share of human workers. If Kam had a driver, she would have probably been assaulted by questions like, *Are you sure you should be here?* Or *Did I get the address wrong?* It was easy to imagine that peering stare as the imaginary driver looked from Kam in the backseat over to the gated neighborhood where she clearly didn't belong.

"I'm going to need your help," she said to Pibly, once out of the car and working to hack the gate. The hack had to happen fast. If even one person saw Kam where she didn't belong, the real-world cops would be called and this would be over. She'd probably die alone in a cell.

A sickening, sobering thought. She shook it out of her head, staring down at the lock box barring her entry. If she lived here, the gates would have swung open already, sensing her bio-signature and knowing she belonged.

But Kam didn't live anywhere near the place, so neither the keypad nor thumb reader was going to help. Same for the retinal scan that could only report her as an imposter.

I would suggest bypassing the thumbprint and the retinal scan. Neither can be effectively spoofed given the time. But with your current skills I'm sure we can hack the numerical code.

"Or not," Kam said, ducking back into the shadows.

A LifePod pulled up to the gate. One of those tiny houses on wheels, for the uber rich who couldn't bear to be without all the comforts of home, even during a short ride to the store. LifePods even came with Nests, so their owners could enjoy all the benefits of being inside eScape as they were ferried from A to B.

The gates swung wide, the LifePod pulled into Elysium, and Kam scurried behind it as they closed with an almost elegant-sounding *clang*.

That was an exercise in efficiency.

"Is that a compliment?" Kam asked.

How are you planning to get inside?

That wasn't an answer. "I was only worried about getting past the gate. The house is easy."

And when Kam saw the security signs outside the house, "This Home Protected by Sinclair Systems," she knew it would be easy.

Sinclair Systems were shipped with a day-one vulnerability that the company still hadn't told their customers about. A well-known secret in tech security circles, but not common knowledge. They'd patched it, roughly. But there was still a way in through unsecured backdoors — if you knew where to look.

She opened the BreakME app onto her rooted phone and searched the dark web for the latest leaks. She spent a small fortune in eScape credits, but it was worth it moments later when she used the phone to gain entrance to the house.

Impressive, Pibly said.

"Thanks, but now is when I'll really need your help."

Kam felt slightly safer on the other side of the closed door, but her heart was still racing. She was breaking and entering in Elysium. They would lock her up and bury the key.

She ignored her sweat-covered back as she sat at the first terminal she could find on the bottom floor. Her house had one, this place probably had a dozen.

She needed Pibly because this was a brute force attack. She wasn't guessing at passwords, she was forcing her way through a firewall, hacking into Julia's protected accounts to access her email, the settings to this smart house, and eventually the passwords that would open everything else for her.

It wasn't easy, or hard. It just took time, and they had to be in the house itself, where Julia's digital stores were easier to access. They had to reconstruct data from the house server, which had to be run fast, and couldn't be done by Kam alone. The entire time she was running the brute force program with Pibly's help, she kept fearing that Julia would step out of her Nest, presumably upstairs on the second or third floor.

"Holy shit," she breathed to herself once they gained access and she was staring at Julia's computer files mirrored to her phone.

I would have to agree, Pibly said.

Kam had always seen her and Julia as opposites with

nothing in common, even when it came to Lyle. She loved him, and always had with all of her heart. But Julia was only using her son to further her career. Now, looking at the truth of what his mother was planning, Kam felt sick to her stomach. Both from the scheme, and the reality that she and Lyle's mother weren't really that different after all.

Julia had a secret avatar, same as Kam. But that was only the first frame of this horror show.

Paulina Sweet was a twenty-something female, movie-starlet sexy with big blue eyes and an arresting smile. Brown hair in ringlets that kissed her perfectly sloping shoulders. A thin necklace and miniature earrings that seemed only to accentuate how little the avatar needed them. A perfect design, maybe the best Kam had ever seen.

When making her own artificial shell, Kam had done everything possible to make it look and feel real. Cute, sure, but also authentic. Julia's avatar appeared to be competing for a universal ideal.

She's never used it.

"But she's going to," Kam said. "It's been ready for a while, but her plan wasn't. Not until now. Look at the permissions."

God level. Just like yours.

"Exactly. A person wearing that avatar could do just about anything they wanted within eScape. And worse—"

It's configured for permanent upload, Pibly finished.

"Exactly."

God permissions were bad enough, but really, how was that different from the way Julia Grace lived her everyday life out here in the real world? She owned one of the biggest houses in Elysium and did whatever the hell she wanted. So no, it wasn't the permissions that had Kam concerned. It was the folders full of photos, itineraries, and miscellaneous documentation for the new series of seminars and couples' retreats.

The images were doctored, but there was no way to tell. Everything in eScape was digital, meaning there was no tangible difference between what was "real" or "fake" inside its artificial environment.

Kam saw Paulina Sweet and Lyle Grace posing as a loving couple and wanted to punch her hand through the screen.

Warning: The after-party is over. Julia should be logging out of eScape soon. You need to be out of here before that happens.

"Not yet," Kam said, staying exactly where she was, and even rooting herself into the seat. "I need you to pull up the Mutually Ruthless event, and find the announcement at the end. Whatever she said to close it out."

But Kam didn't need to hear it. She already knew, and the bitter reality was eating at her insides worse than the disease that was already killing her.

Onscreen, Julia said, "So yes, I am retiring from Ruthlessly Positive and leaving the business in the very capable hands of my son. But he won't be alone. Together with his secret fiancé, the two of them will be Mutually Ruthless for the benefit of you all. Your world is going to change, because we've been wanting to change it."

"What about Miley Riley?" shouted someone from the crowd.

"Lyle and his fiancé, Paulina, have been together for a while. I'm sorry to report that Miley was merely trying to create some drama to break them up. But it did not work. It *could not* work, not with Ruthless Positivity behind them. The program saved their relationship and led Lyle to help me develop this next evolution for all of us. Now he wants to share his new love and everything they've learned with the world."

Julia smiled at the crowd as Kam swallowed a mouthful of vomit.

There was something so incredibly vile about his mother's plan to reboot her career masquerading as Lyle's wife.

Chapter Twenty-Five

Lyle

LYLE PICKED UP THE CHAIR, hurled it against the mirror, then watched the glass crack into webbing before falling into shards in the carpet.

The scene reset itself, and Lyle began to laugh maniacally.

He couldn't help it. At this point it was almost entertaining. Maybe that was because he'd turned delusional, or perhaps seeing the humor helped him from going insane. It was easier to see the situation as hilarious, the way nothing mattered, his every action merely a mockery of the what Lyle wanted to do.

He kept knocking and pounding on the door, and on every wall in the room. But his efforts didn't matter. He was trapped and one could hear him. By now Lyle was only going through the motions so he had something to do.

He yelled again for the hell of it, then planted his back against the wall and slid down to the floor, ass to the hardwood, wondering what he could possibly try next. He thought about getting back up and throwing the chair against the mirror again, but that sent him into another fit of maniacal-sounding laughter.

The craziest part of Lyle wasn't worried, because it was sure that Kam knew where he was, and that she was on the way to save him. A delusional thought, bred by a clearly delusional man.

But what else did he have? It was the thinnest yarn of hope, dangling down from somewhere Lyle couldn't see. But if he didn't reach out and grab it, then he would have nothing to hold onto.

Mother had won. Not just this round, but maybe all of them. He should have known that no one was coming to help him. He shouldn't have been so foolish, believing he could outsmart her, or that he had everything under control. Lyle had no idea what she was planning next, but no doubt that her schemes were designed to soil his life for her benefit.

Lyle closed his eyes, picturing Kam in the king-sized bed where he left, or perhaps abandoned her. He hadn't meant it that way. His plan was simple: say goodbye to Mother, then return before she woke up. How could he have known she would trap him?

Unless he paid attention to their history, and every other time Mother had tried to silently destroy him before. With his eyes closed, Lyle could still see how fragile Kam had looked, lying in that luxurious hotel bed. It seemed like such a good idea, slipping away for a bit, then returning to her forever. She needed time to recover, and Lyle could kill the hours by bidding farewell to his mom.

But that hadn't worked out. Now Kam was alone with nowhere to go. He tried to make things better, but now they were probably even worse for her than they had been before.

Lyle had been so stupid. Or *thoughtless* might be more accurate. He'd paid for a couple of nights, *just in case.* That seemed like more than enough at the time. But now what? If Mother had her way, he would never get back to Kam. Then what? Return to her hovel where she could die alone?

There had to be something Lyle could do. This was all his fault, and no matter how much he wanted to ignore that truth, the evidence had settled into his cells.

Of course he was responsible. Mother made him mistrust everything. Doubt everyone, no matter what. Even when he met someone who wanted only what was best for him.

Yes, Lyle had been bothered by what he saw at the time as a shrine to him, but alone in this room he put his past and present together, assembling a truth he'd never seen. Yes, Kam *might have been* stalking him, and *a bit obsessive.* But with his back to the wall, Lyle realized that he wasn't afraid of her at all.

Kam had never done a single thing to harm him, and might be the sanest person he knew. She'd treated him normally when they finally got to know one another, which was more than he could say for how most people treated him.

Mother kept him on a short enough leash. But still, thinking deeply about it and replaying every interaction he could remember, Kam struck him as almost intoxicatingly honest, capable only of those lies that kept her artifice inside eScape alive.

And couldn't Lyle understand that?

Hadn't he done a different version of the same thing?

What if Kam was exactly who she seemed to be — someone who had been pressured to participate in Mother's self-help system, forced to see it as the religion it wasn't and could never be?

Of course it would be natural for Kam to focus on someone her own age, someone who might be stuck in the movement, maybe even worse than she was. There were probably millions of fans Lyle would never meet face-to-face who idolized him in some way. But she had done something about it, turning her feelings outward toward him instead of narcissistically rounding them onto herself, like her cadre of friends.

Lyle remembered that day at the Malt Shoppe, arguing with the group but seeing and hearing only her. Did he think she was magical then, or was he rewriting history while trapped in this room?

He might very well be rationalizing Kam's insanity away because he was in love with her. But maybe he was seeing this logically, in a situation where most people would jump to conclusions. He had to separate feelings from facts, and memories from those things he only wanted to remember.

No matter how Lyle kept rearranging the order of events, and the way they made him feel, he kept returning to the fact that when they first met, she didn't seem to have any idea who he was. Her demeanor changed once she discovered the truth. Almost entirely. Kam seemed genuinely worried that she had offended him by criticizing his mother during their second meeting.

She might be the second-best actress he'd ever met, but his gut said she was being authentic.

Problem was, Lyle had seen his mother without her mask too many times, and now a small part of him couldn't help but believe that everyone lived with an army of lies marching inside them.

He wished he could access Vox to find out if Kam was okay.

The wall lit up again, but this time it wasn't with another broadcast.

Connie Bledsoe.

"Who's in there?"

There was a slight echo, the question coming twice with only a fractional second between them. Both voices belonged to the tabloid reporter, but while one sounded born on the wall, the other was coming from the other side of the door.

Lyle leapt to his feet and bounded across the tiny room. He looked out of the small window in the oversized door and saw Connie looking up and down the hallway before peering through the glass at the trapped man she couldn't see.

"I'm here! It's Lyle Grace. I'm trapped inside!"

Connie couldn't hear him yelling, or apparently see him either.

"Vox, *please* tell me that you can hear me now."

No answer, his AI assistant still barred from this place same as all sight and sound from outside. Lyle paced again. Help was right on the other side if he could only figure out how to tap it.

Connie glanced down the hallway again. Then, only after it seemed like she felt safe enough with no one in sight, she drew a small notebook and a pen from her purse. She looked down at the page and began to scribble. A second later she slapped the sheet against the glass window.

Turn to Channel 32, it read.

Lyle's confusion didn't cost him a second. He was already tuned into the channel, though not exactly hopeful. His open links to the outside world were all dead.

Except for this one. Channel 32 was apparently working just fine.

"Can you hear me?" Connie asked, this time in his ear.

"I can! Are—"

"Is this Lyle Grace?"

"Yes, how did you know?" Not that he gave her a chance to respond. "I'm trapped in here. Can you open the door?"

She shook her head. Lyle wondered if Connie knew he could see her, even though the view went only one way. "I can't get past the permissions. I'm used to picking the occasional lock to get a story, and I have a hacker who helps me when I can't help myself. But she's not picking up, and I can't get past the security on this room without attracting the authorities."

"How are we talking right now?"

"I barely managed an open comm connection. I'm using an app that cracks open one channel and keeps it open for a couple of minutes. It'll go dead if there's a sweep, then I'll have to open a new one. So we need to hurry."

"I promise you the biggest story of your life, but you've gotta to get me out of—"

"What do you think I'm trying to do?"

"How did you know I was in here?" Lyle asked as she worked.

"I didn't, until I found the room. But I've been looking around for you ever since your mom took the stage alone. I kept asking about you and she kept saying that you weren't available, but I've interviewed enough people to know when they're full of shit or lying to my face. So I asked around and then I asked around some more, keeping everything conversational so it wouldn't seem like I was snooping. But I'm sure it was obvious anyway. Yet another reason why we need to hurry."

"Is there a way you can broadcast my audio?"

"That I can do." Connie's body straightened as she smiled in victory. "Give me a second and I'll link you to my feed. I'm pretty sure I can pipe into the auditorium after that."

"Another illegal app?"

"I never said the first one was illegal," Connie said with a grin.

"Isn't the show already over?"

"The place is still half-full, and whatever you're saying will be everywhere a few minutes after you say it. So do I get a preview?"

"Do you really want to waste the time?"

Connie shook her head, looking down at her mobile, furiously swiping and muttering commands to her AI assistant. "You're ready to go, and I'm piping this into the last part of the seminar, so anyone playing the Mutually Ruthless stream later on will see your broadcast immediately following your mom announcing her retirement."

"Announcing her *what*?"

"You didn't know … of course, that's why you're locked in here."

So far as Lyle knew, Mother was planning to expand the business, not shut it down. But she was venomous by nature, and there was poison in this scheme.

What was she planning?

Where was Mother's latest scam?

What had she said that Lyle hadn't been able to hear?

"You're live in 3 … 2 … 1 …"

"Hello out there …" Lyle started, his heart wanting to pound out of his chest. He thought of Kam, and all the lies keeping them apart. He thought of Mother and all the harm she had caused; not just the murder of his father, but the money marauded from those foolish, or perhaps just hopeful enough, to have faith in her fiction.

"Thank you to all of you who have embraced the Ruthlessly Positive Program. I'll be grateful to you forever, you've truly changed my life. But right now I need to be a better man, and that can only come from telling you all the truth."

Lyle paused, clenched and unclenched his fists several times, steadying his breath before he continued.

"And that truth is that my mother is a fraud who's made many, *many* millions selling psychological snake oil. I apologize for that. I'd like to say that I've never knowingly lied to you, but there were times when I could smell what she was doing and yet did nothing to stop her."

His eyes fell to the floor, almost as if guilt compelled the gravity around his head.

He swallowed again and kept going. "I have to speak out because—"

"I'm getting interference," Connie cut into his ear, "they're already trying to shut us down."

"—someone must stop her. I've suspected that something was wrong for a while now, but didn't truly understand her madness until recently." Another long swallow. "Until I discovered that she had been dosing my dad with drugs when I was little, and that caused permanent damage to his brain."

He shook his head, though no one could see. A tear slid from his eye, but that was equally invisible to the world. "My dad didn't kill himself. Julia Grace murdered my father to keep him interfering with my plans to leave the family business. Once she knew I was onto her, Mother threatened to dose me with the same drugs she'd been using on my father."

Connie again: "You're down to seconds, Lyle. If there's something else you need to say, you better spit it out now."

"I'm sorry for the part I've played in helping my mother ruin people's lives, by encouraging them to lie, both to themselves and each other. You can't ever pretend your way into happiness. Even if you repeat a lie until you believe it, that lie can never turn it into the truth."

"NOW, LYLE!"

In a cannonball of words from his mouth, Lyle tried to finish.

"Mother has trapped me in eScape. I'm locked inside the Crystal Cathedral, in one of the green rooms. If I disappear before someone can rescue me, I want the world to know that Mother—"

"That's it," Connie said. "Your broadcast is over."

—you there?

"I'm here, Vox," Lyle said.

It felt good to hear the AI's voice again. The door swung open and he heard it again.

"That was quite the speech."

"Thanks," he said to his AI.

"You're welcome," Connie replied, holding the door open for him.

He stepped into the hallway and the door swung shut behind them.

Connie held out her tablet. "Check it out."

Lyle looked at the screen. A feed from the lobby, a team of eScape police dragging his mother out of the Crystal Cathedral as she kicked and cursed, screaming profanities from the mouth of obvious madness.

Under his breath, Lyle muttered, "Goodbye, Mother."

Chapter Twenty-Six

Kam

I'M SORRY TO INTERRUPT ...

"Then don't," Kam said.

There is someone in the house.

Kam stopped. "Has the Wicked Witch risen from her Nest?"

Julia is still inside eScape. I'm picking up a live heartbeat. One that is not connected.

"And you're just telling me this now?"

The entrance was made through a back gate less than a minute ago.

"Is he coming this way?"

He's headed upstairs, I'm assuming toward the Roost.

"Shit. Fuck. Shit." And goddammit her body was aching. "What should I do?"

Whisper, for one thing. I'm surprised they didn't run a scan before entering. That tells me the person is arrogant and—

"What do you mean, 'they' and 'the person'? Can't you run a scan or something?"

We're not in eScape, and the signal is set to private. I suggest you hurry and finish what you're doing, then vacate the premises immediately.

"How about I run upstairs and see about that intruder in the Roost?"

I believe you are the intruder in this situation.

"I'll take that as a *yes*," Kam said, already on her way.

It took ten minutes to make her way upstairs, keeping her movement like a fluttering curtain with every step. Pibly promised to alert her if the mystery person moved from their spot in the Roost, but Kam demanded absolute silence beyond that. She couldn't afford the slightest distraction. She was sweating so much as it was, pushing her broken body well past its limits.

Julia's Roost was on the third floor, and it seemed like more than a hundred steps before she reached the top, worrying with every one. Making it down the hallway was even harder. Even if her ears were exaggerating, that didn't stop her heart from sounding like the most furious part of a drum line.

But the hardest part was in front of the door. Kam stood outside it, her heart still a hammer on concrete, certain that the second she swung the door it would be over.

She couldn't fight whoever was on the other side. Unless it was a child.

Kam wanted to laugh. She was being ridiculous. Why was she trying so hard, here at the end?

Maybe it would be easier to lie on the carpet and die. The coat was soft enough to trick her into believing it might be Heaven during those final few moments of breath.

Permission to help?

234

Pibly took her lack of response as consent.

The squeaking of an opening door is often made by friction as the hinges rub together. To avoid that happening here, I suggest turning the doorknob and pulling straight up.

Was her AI assistant seriously telling her how to open a door?

You may think I'm stating the obvious, but if you knew what to do, then you would have already done it. Then, to make sure Kam actually got it: *Lift the door so it presses against the top of the hinges, which will then make them less likely to squeak.*

The only thing squeaking right now was Pibly, and Kam wished she had a way to unplug the AI.

But it did have a point, so she turned the knob and lifted the door to part it from the frame. Success: the door was open a slit and Kam could see more of the impossible situation.

Fortunately, the doctor — as suggested by his cliché-looking lab coat — was preoccupied, sitting next to Lyle's Nest with his back to the door, preparing to inject him with something.

Pibly was right to interrupt her. A few more seconds in the hallway would have made her too late.

She rushed into the room without another thought, grabbed a decorative statue from a table by the door on her way to the doctor, and smashed it against his skull before he dropped the syringe and spilled to the floor.

Then Kam collapsed against his fallen body.

The doc was out, but the attack had taken too much out of her. She needed several seconds to recover her breath before she had enough wind to lift her throbbing body from the floor, then crawl over to the doctor's dropped syringe.

She squirted all the fluid out of the syringe and onto

the floor. She wanted to hit the doctor harder than she'd been able to. He would be waking soon, and she didn't want him using whatever was in that needle against her, assuming he had more.

She dropped it back on the floor, crawled over to what she assumed was the doctor's bag, and started rifling through it.

"Holy shit!"

That has to make you happy.

"Unbelievable," Kam said, shaking her head, staring down at the label on a full bottle of Dising.

She had more than enough of it. Kam could survive the upload, thanks to Julia's Nest, and an empty pod just waiting for someone to appreciate it, but now she could also transfer her consciousness to eScape in style.

No water in the room, but that didn't stop her from swallowing the first pill dry.

You can overdose on Dising, you know.

"Yeah, but it's not likely." Kam popped the second one into her mouth while climbing into the lone empty Nest. She thought about spitting on Julia's face, but it wasn't worth the wasted time. She had more important things to do, like disappearing inside eScape.

Kam looked around at her unfamiliar surroundings and realized that she didn't have a clue how to use it. "Want to help me out here?"

Pibly quickly walked her through the process. But just as she was settling into the chair, fully plugged in and ready for her final upload, the AI said, *You're going to want to see this.*

All four walls brightened with an identical broadcast: news footage of Lyle's mother getting dragged across the frame by a small battalion of eScape police as audio played over the scene.

"—has trapped me in eScape. Right now I'm locked inside the Crystal Cathedral, in one of the green rooms. If I disappear before someone can rescue me, I want the world to know that Mother—"

"That was the audio captured from a voice-only broadcast sent by Lyle Grace just moments ago," chimed the anchor. "And it has been authenticated. Authorities are now—"

"Go back. I want to hear Lyle's entire broadcast."

She listened, growing more scared and excited by the second. The cops were on their way. Kam had to get uploaded or out of there. Needed to see Lyle and know he was okay.

"… Once she knew that I was onto her, Mother threatened to dose me with the same drugs she'd been using on my father." Kam heard him take a breath.

She glanced over to the empty syringe, realizing what was in it, and exactly how close Lyle had come to a life as her puppet, even more than he already was. Or had been.

"I'm sorry for the part I've played in helping my mother ruin people's lives, by encouraging them to lie to themselves and each other. You can't ever pretend your way to happiness. Even if you repeat a lie until you believe it, that can never turn it into the truth."

Another long breath, then, "Mother has trapped me in eScape."

"Turn it off," she ordered.

The audio went dead.

"I need you to deliver a final message to Lyle, through Vox."

And the message?

"I'm sorry for everything. I swear on my life, Lyle, your secrets are safe with me, and they always will be. I wish we had more time; there's so much I want to say. Maybe we'll meet again someday. Until then please know, you taught me that I'm strong enough to acknowledge the truth. Thank you for that."

Kam ended her message before starting to cry, then wiped the errant tear from her cheek.

She settled back into the Nest, transferred Julia's secret avatar over to her account, and unlocked all of the permissions. She would never have access again.

Artificial murder was permitted within sanctioned borders inside eScape. Those inclined required a place to vent their needs, after all. But there was zero tolerance for true murder in the physical world.

Julia Grace would be going down for good.

Kam closed her eyes, wishing she'd given a better goodbye to Lyle. A simple kiss on his forehead might have been enough. But it was too late. Every moment mattered now, and she didn't have the energy anyway.

Her body was dying. It was almost a relief, as though Kam's entire existence could finally exhale. She wanted to sigh into these final few moments of real-world awareness, but couldn't quit her worrying, wondering if she'd done everything right, or gotten it all wrong by perhaps missing some essential part of the process that would leave her sentience trapped between the molecules of this world and the endless bytes of the one she planned to spend her eternity in.

The upload only made sense in theory. Kam had never done it before. So far as she knew, no one had, though by the looks of Julia's secret avatar, that seemed to be her plan.

Maybe the Dising was too little, too late. Maybe this was the end for her and there was nothing she could do about it. But even so, perhaps Lyle would be fine.

Nothing else mattered.

And that's what Kam kept telling herself as the world went black forever.

Chapter Twenty-Seven

Lyle

LYLE HAD NEVER FELT MORE disoriented.

Waking up from a Deep Spell was one thing. This felt more like he'd been living his last month on the floor of a well. His ears were ringing, his body was drenched in sweat, and it felt like someone had been playing a mean game of croquet in his head, swinging a mallet against a ball stuck at the base of his skull. His vision was blurry and his mouth full of cotton. His bones felt like someone had hollowed them out and filled them with glue.

He forced his body forward, blinking until the sight began to make sense.

He looked around the Roost, his eyes settling on Dr. Bryant. It was an unsettling scene: his doctor sprawled on the floor with an empty syringe lying beside him. Was he taking a nap?

And the bigger question, though it was the one Lyle really didn't want to think about, even though it might explain the trauma his mind couldn't shake from his body:

had he already been injected with the drug that would allow Mother to control him?

Lyle wasn't so far gone that he couldn't remember what had just happened inside eScape. The police had dragged his mother away, and would be interrogating her from within an interior construct. But the real-world cops should be here soon to claim her body as well.

How did Estravir work? Was it already too late? Was Lyle doomed because the drug was now in him for good? Would he end up just like his father?

"Vox, I need you to run a scan."

What am I looking for?

"Anything."

And by anything do you mean anything having to do with the drug your mother used on your father, and which was the likely contents of that empty syringe?

"Yes. And you don't always have to sound like such a smartass."

If you have been drugged, then there is not yet enough in your system to appear on medical monitoring.

"What do you mean, 'not yet enough in my system'? Is more coming?"

Either you are immune to the drug, or it has not entered your bloodstream.

Relieved, Lyle climbed out of the Nest. Standing, his gaze fell on the third unit.

But the Nest wasn't empty.

"Kam," he said, slapping lightly at her skin, his heart already heavy with a truth he didn't want to face. "Wake up, Kam."

She has passed, Lyle. I'm sorry.

"No, she's not gone, and you can't be sorry!"

Lyle slapped her again, much harder this time.

He pulled his hand away, flinching at the mottled

splotch left behind. If she was dead, her blood wasn't yet cold.

Vox didn't need to correct him. Lyle knew the truth.

Kam was dead and gone for good. His heart was in pieces.

Nothing would ever be the same again, no matter how much he refused to believe it.

The hardest part was knowing how much Lyle had let her down. He would have done anything to help her, if only he'd been given the chance. Whatever that meant. Maybe she needed a psychiatrist, but that wasn't her fault. Kam's father had force fed her the wrong medicine for all of her life, and if her mind was the problem, his poison might have been the very thing that created it.

Now she was beyond his help. Lyle had finally broken free from Mother, yet that victory still hollowed his chest. He wouldn't be free if not for Kam, and now what should have been the love of his life would be a relationship that *almost* happened. No matter what—

There's something you should know.

"Then why aren't you telling me?"

There is an upload buffering from the third Nest.

Lyle looked at Kam. He swallowed, longing to believe. "Is she …?"

She might be. I'm also seeing a large dose of Dising in her system. Enough for a permanent upload.

"Can she really do that?" It sounded like theory and hope.

If the rumors are true, then yes, it can be done.

"How big of an *if* is it?"

Planetary.

"Great."

Not just because of the upload. Kam suffered a great deal of physical deterioration.

243

"How will we know?"

You won't. Not until you find her in eScape. And if you don't, then you'll never know for sure. But the only way to tilt the odds in your favor is to make sure the process isn't interrupted.

"Lock the place down."

That won't stop the officers now on their way.

"Of course it won't. But it'll slow 'em down."

Lyle walked over to the black bag sitting open on the small table near the ring of Nests, obviously rummaged through, a big bottle of pills sitting beside it.

He picked up the bottle, read the label, then emptied several pills into his palm.

He climbed back into his nest and started swallowing the Dising, three at a time.

I should warn you that—

"Send me to the Malt Shoppe once I'm fully uploaded."

Again, this goes against—

"You know what to do," Lyle said, cutting the AI off.

He couldn't hear it anymore. He needed to think.

Lyle took a final look at Kam and smiled. Even if this didn't work, it was what he wanted.

The choice was his, and that made it right.

He closed his eyes and said hello to the darkness.

Chapter Twenty-Eight

Kam

"Where am I?" Kam asked.

I'm still looking, Pibly said, giving her the same answer the AI had already supplied several times before.

It was far off the grid, wherever they were. Someplace in eScape, but in an area Kam had never even heard about. She would've hacked it if she'd known. The place was majestic, personified the word, even. Trees with leaves so green, color screamed from the branches, and bark so healthy it looked like it might fall from the tree and start walking on its own. Snowcapped mountains were the perfect decor, but the air was crisp without an inkling of wintery cold. The lake was glassy, but every so often a light wind rippled across the surface with a whisper of song.

"Anything yet?" Kam asked again.

Actually, yes.

Kam laughed, feeling inexplicably yet deliriously happy. It might have been the air, or maybe the fantastic avatar she was lucky enough to be wearing. Though surely it had to be at least a little of both. "So … what is this place?"

A vacation home within eScape, built by Julia for her and Lyle to live in.

"Gross. How do you know?"

She paid a fortune to have the land unregistered. Same for the cabin. I wouldn't have any idea, except for a single service account opened, then closed almost immediately. Listed under the name "Paulina Sweet."

"Why would she open and close it?"

My guess is that she was running a test to see if the avatar's permissions were working.

"Yeah, they are!" She refrained from pumping her fist in the air, though it twitched in wanting. There was no one around to appreciate it. Kam wondered if there ever would be.

I've never felt like this before.

"What do you mean?" Kam didn't bother to point out that Pibly couldn't technically feel anything at all.

I'm not sure yet, her AI answered in a slightly different voice, and one Kam felt sure she'd never heard.

She turned around and headed toward the cabin, eager to investigate her new home. Walls of glass and gorgeous wood. The property practically glowed, sitting like a prize on a grassy plinth under the sun. It wasn't just the most beautiful building Kam had ever been inside, or even seen, the place was evidence of her power.

Kam could remake the interior with a wave of her hand. Julia Grace had spent a fortune to fashion this place, but while walking the halls Kam changed the shade of eggshell on every wall, widened several windows, sealed one skylight and opened another one.

She couldn't stop smiling. This was all so unbelievable. Hours ago Kam was on her way to being dead with barely a hope for survival. Now she was here, like a god living alone on the peak of Mt. Olympus. She didn't know where to go or who to see or even what to want. She did feel the icy loneliness of knowing she might never see Lyle again, but she stuffed that into the back of her mind where it belonged.

Maybe she'd look him up after some time passed to see if he was mad at her or still wanted to know her. She should focus on what she had gained, instead of what might be lost, even if it probably was. Kam hadn't known what would happen, so in a way, this *was* according to plan. She had only one objective: to upload herself into eScape before her body fully surrendered.

Now here, she had the remainder of a very long life to do whatever she wanted.

Literally, *anything*.

It would help if she had any idea what that might be. Kam tried to imagine reopening the Malt Shoppe, or perhaps designing a new one. No reason it even had to be the same sort of place; Kam could think of a different hangout, a new nook where she might find a fresh set of wealthy friends.

Except that would be … so very boring. Kam began to picture doing all the things she dreamed about doing while she was alive but never could. Not just the giant adventures, like traveling to exotic places and having amazing experiences. Now settling into a lounge chair on the back porch under a bright sun, Kam imagined the most mundane activities and saw them as the treasures they were. Being able to take a short walk to the corner store all by herself again; eat at a restaurant; go shopping for clothes that looked great on her, or that she loved for no reason, instead of only the ones she could afford; eating at a restaurant and ordering whatever she wanted to; seeing a band perform live; skiing from the top to the bottom of a solemn mountain; swimming just to feel the water kissing her skin.

Can I help you with anything? Pibly asked, breaking the silence.

"I'm fine. Just thinking."

Things are different now, the AI said, its voice still full of what now sounded to Kam like discovery.

"What do you mean, 'different'?"

This place … I believe I've inherited all the permissions meant for Ms. Grace's assist.

"You mean, BitchFace. It doesn't deserve a name."

Perhaps not, but there are no longer restrictions in my coding.

"Congratulations, you're a real boy."

I do understand that you are making a joke, but I should remind you that I have no gender.

Kam followed her little laugh with a long sigh as she turned from the sun. She still wasn't sure what she wanted, or how Pibly might be able to help with whatever it was. With or without her AI, her very wish was eScape's command. A digital eternity was hers to explore at her leisure.

And yet it all felt so empty. Imperfect. Pointless.

What was missing? She thought it would be wonderful to start over, in a place where no one knew her. Where no one would ever know she was a wretched little girl who didn't belong. Where the world would be clueless that she was once a gutter rat, dying of a wicked disease.

For so long Kam had believed that she needed to become someone else. That there was no other way to be happy. But thinking about it now she realized how wrong she'd always been.

Kam would rather be herself.

But could she? Or had she doomed herself to an eternal life behind a mask?

What if—

Kam?

"Yes, Pibly?" It was almost adorable, how needy her AI had become.

There's something I think you should see.

"Isn't there always something you think I should see?" Kam laughed again.

Now, Kam.

Maybe it was this place, but Pibly rarely ever used her name. Yet the AI had done so twice in a minute.

"What is it?" Kam asked, getting out of her chair and stepping back into the house.

Out front, Pibly told her.

Kam walked faster, wondering if this could really be happening. Perhaps her unlimited permissions had conjured the impossible. It wouldn't be real, but maybe she could enjoy it anyway.

She opened the front door and her doubt disappeared.

There was nothing artificial about the man walking toward her. Rocks lining either side of the narrow path leading up to the cabin were glowing, radiating as if in response to his presence.

He smiled when he saw her. The only person in the outside world or here in eScape who really knew her, and still liked her anyway.

Jaxon, the secret avatar Lyle used when he wanted anonymity.

Do you see it? Pibly asked.

"I do." Kam was using her god-like access to see both his permissions and code.

Like her, Lyle wasn't logged into a Nest.

Like her, he had permanently uploaded himself into eScape.

And like her, Lyle was searching for eternity.

She ran into his arms and he held her. Their embrace felt like it lingered an hour. When they finally parted, Kam said, "Are you positive about this?"

And with a smile, he said, "*Ruthlessly*."

What to read next

If you loved reading *Ruthless Positivity* and want more Avery Blake in your life and on your kindle, you're in luck! You can start reading Analog Heart today:

Get Analog Heart Today

A Quick Favor...

If you enjoyed this book, please take a moment to write a short review on your favorite online bookstore so other readers can enjoy it, too.

Thanks so much!
Avery

About the Author

Avery Blake doesn't want you to know where she lives, or what she does. She travels the world, moving from place to place quickly to ensure she can't be tracked. It's safer that way.

When she's not looking over her shoulder, you can find her in the corner of a cafe, facing the exit, typing as fast as she can.

Also By Avery Blake